PAYTON AND THE PASSIONATE PARTISAN

ANNA MARKLAND

PAYTON AND THE PASSIONATE PARTISAN
BY
ANNA MARKLAND
©2024

Dedicated to the people of Spain

*If penicillin can cure those that are ill,
Spanish sherry can bring the dead back to life.
~Sir Alexander Fleming*

*"There will always be time enough to die. A drowning man will instinctively clutch at a straw. It is the natural law of the moral world that a nation that finds itself on the brink of an abyss will try to save itself by any means.
~Carl Von Clausewitz*

Payton and the Passionate Partisan by Anna Markland

Book Two, Highland Whisky Kings

© 2024 Anna Markland

All rights reserved. This book is licensed for your personal enjoyment only. It may not be re-sold or given away to other people. If you would like to share this book with another person, please purchase an additional copy for each recipient. Thank you for respecting the hard work of this author. This book or parts thereof may not be reproduced in any form, stored in any retrieval system, or transmitted in any form by any means—electronic, mechanical, photocopy, recording, or otherwise—without prior written permission of the publisher, except as provided by United States of America copyright law.

This is a work of fiction. Names, characters, places, and incidents either are the products of the author's imagination or are used fictitiously. Any resemblance to actual persons, living or dead, businesses, companies, events, or locales is entirely coincidental.

Cover by Dar Albert

MORE ANNA MARKLAND

Anna is a USA Today bestseller who has authored more than sixty award-winning and much-loved Medieval, Viking, Highlander, Elizabethan and Regency historical romances. No matter the historical or geographic setting, many of her series recount the adventures of successive generations of one family, with emphasis on the importance of ancestry and honor. A detailed list with links can be found at
https://www.annamarkland.com/
She is an independent author, so getting the word out about her book is vital to its success. If you enjoy this book, please consider writing a review. Reviews help other readers find stories to enjoy.

OVER A BARREL

Payton King nuzzled his fiancée's ear. "In short, Miss Foxworthy," he whispered, "the French have us o'er a barrel."

Frowning, she pulled away.

He might have known Jasmine wouldn't understand the pun. Then again, when he'd attempted the jest earlier in the day at the offices of the Duke of Withenshawe's shipping company, none of the duke's employees had caught on.

"Barrel, ye see," he explained. "We canna get our barrels back from Spain because Bonaparte is laying siege to Cádiz."

"Cádiz?"

He sometimes wondered if she ever listened to a word he said. "It's a port. The closest to the sherry distillery in Jerez where we sent our staves."

"Tell me about that again," she said.

Payton's cousin, Kenneth, Duke of Ramsay, had told him of a trick he often used to avoid reacting negatively to another person's obtuseness. Payton had found it quite useful, especially when dealing with Jasmine. She always seemed to have her mind elsewhere when he talked about his family's distillery in the Scottish Highlands. So, he counted to ten before he replied. "Five year gone, we made barrel staves using an age-old method handed down from the Vikings."

"Five years ago," she corrected, shuddering as she usually did when he mentioned Vikings. She'd refused to believe his assertion that many Highlanders, himself included, were descendants of the Norsemen. "How can that be true, silly man?" she'd replied. "You don't speak Norwegian or Danish."

He should be used to having his grammar corrected by now, so he counted to ten again and resumed his explanation. "We sent the staves to Spain where they made them into barrels to store sherry."

"So, why do you want them back if they are full of sherry? Your distillery doesn't produce sherry, does it?"

Seated in a distant corner of the library of Ramsay House, Niven snorted. Supposedly immersed in a book, the youngest King brother had so far kept silent and Payton admired his restraint.

"No, we distill the finest single malt whisky in the world," he replied, realizing that counting to ten wasn't calming his impatience. "The barrels will be empty when we retrieve them but the sherry will have permeated the wood, and..."

"I suppose that's the reason the Regent granted you a Royal Warrant," she said. "Making a whisky he likes, I mean."

Perhaps she did listen sometimes, but he worried about taking her to Scotland when they married. She'd not fare well there if she insisted on the family speaking the King's English and not the Kings' English. He'd considered sharing that witty pun with her, but she didn't take well to any hint of criticism. She'd dropped a few hints about staying in England, but that wasn't an option for him.

He was relieved when Kenneth's sister entered the library. He'd once thought he and Daisy might make a go of it, but some folk said that marrying a cousin wasn't a good idea and Daisy wasn't his type anyway—too sullen and unpredictable. She'd once led him on then dumped him for no good reason.

"Ready?" Daisy asked Jasmine.

The two women had never been friends, so it was good of Daisy to take Jasmine under her wing. An afternoon of exploring the Bond Street shops was planned.

"Ye've more patience than me," Niven remarked with a sigh after the ladies had left.

"Than I," he pointed out. "*Crivvens*! I'm getting to be as bad as she is."

"But ye love the lass."

"Aye. Nothin' to be done about it now."

A year ago, in the first flush of their liaison, he'd been besotted and proposed marriage.

"Do ye remember how we used to do everything in our power to avoid the parson's noose when we were lads?" Niven asked. "Now, Tavish is happily wed to Piper and livin' in the Highlands doin' what he loves."

"Aye, and they've birthed a wee bairn."

"I suppose seeing our older brother's happiness when he married Piper affected my judgment," Payton remarked, suddenly feeling homesick. "I thought I'd found my soulmate. It would be dishonorable to renege now and, in any case, I do love Jasmine, despite that she tends to be a featherbrain."

"Weel, when ye marry, ye can always find consolation in her tempting physical attributes," Niven suggested.

Payton would never admit it, but Jasmine's magnificent breasts were the main reason for his original besottedness. He lived in hopes that, one day, she might allow him to...

"Let's away for a ride in Hyde Park," he declared when his manhood stirred. "We can clear our heads and ponder the problem o' the barrels."

NIVEN MIGHT HAVE TEASED his brother. He knew only too well why Payton wanted to get some fresh air and cool off. However, he was worried. When older brother Tavish met Piper Graham, it was plain to anyone with eyes that they were meant for each other. Jasmine and Payton had lost that spark and Niven feared the original attraction may have been purely physical. Payton tended to lose his ability to think rationally in the face of a tempting pair of globes.

Jasmine truly was a scatterbrain, though Niven sometimes suspected she deliberately showed no interest in the family business. Her haughty indifference might lead a fellow to believe she belonged to a rich, aristocratic family. The opposite was true. Her father hailed from gentry but he had gambled away most of their money.

After their wedding, Tavish and his bride returned to Glengeárr. Payton and Niven stayed behind in England to oversee the plans to ship *Uachdaran* whisky by sea from Dundee to London and to secure warehouse space for storage. However, the plan was always to return to Scotland. At least, Niven hoped that was still the plan. He didn't have much confidence in Jasmine warming to the Highlands, but suspected Payton missed their home as much as he did.

Quite by accident, Niven had discovered that Payton had volunteered to sail to Spain if there proved to be no other way to retrieve the barrels. The knot in his gut tightened when he thought of his brother going off to war-torn Spain. It was hurtful that Payton hadn't confided in him, nor sought his opinion of the idea.

Uachdaran was a fine single malt without the added hint of flavor the sherry barrels would provide. The three brothers had always been close, a team united against their abusive parents. Tavish would be disappointed if his brainchild didn't come to fruition, but might never recover if Payton lost his life in an attempt to retrieve the barrels.

Jasmine enjoyed traveling in the Hawkins' well-sprung carriage, though it meant enduring meaningless chit-chat with Daisy, a woman she'd never liked.

At least whisky wasn't the topic of conversation. Jasmine wished she could summon more enthusiasm for Payton's passion for whisky. But really, what was so wonderful about the vile tasting brew?

"Are you looking forward to living in the Highlands?" Daisy suddenly asked.

Jasmine would have to tread carefully. Her traveling companion and Payton were cousins and she didn't trust Daisy at all. "Oh, yes," she lied. "I can't wait to see the distillery for myself."

In truth, the prospect of living among a whole village full of people whose lives revolved around whisky filled her with dread. Even the thought of living in a small village churned her stomach. She'd have to convince Payton to stay in London after they married.

SHOPPING

Jasmine always felt uneasy around Daisy Hawkins, and not because the woman was the sister of the Duke of Ramsay. This sudden interest in shopping expeditions stood in sharp contrast to the mutual dislike they'd felt since childhood. Daisy was well aware that the Foxworthys teetered on the edge of financial ruin—probably the reason she'd suggested shopping on London's most expensive street.

There was no doubt Daisy had deliberately thrown Jasmine and Payton King together. Did she regret it now? If her ploy was to drive a wedge between them, she'd better think again. A Highlander who distilled whisky might not be the kind of husband Jasmine had envisioned for herself, but the Regent's royal warrant apparently had the potential to turn the Kings into rich men. And the broad-shouldered, well-muscled Payton was certainly easy on the eye.

"I really don't need another pair of gloves," Daisy

whined after she'd spent half an hour perusing the wares in a haberdashery. "But these are so darling."

Since Kenneth Hawkins, Duke of Ramsay, had returned from Scotland months ago, there'd been no entertainment and no visitors at Ramsay House. His sister, Daisy, often boasted of her dislike of horse riding, so it was unlikely she would have any occasion to wear the extravagant burgundy kidskin gloves she was holding.

Kenneth probably missed his mother who'd decided to stay in Scotland. That was surely the reason for his morose demeanor and hermit lifestyle. He certainly wasn't the jovial fellow he used to be. Perhaps Daisy had an explanation. "Is your brother feeling better?" she asked.

"He isn't ill," Daisy replied. "Not that it's any of your business."

There'd been none of the usual rancor up to this point, so Jasmine assumed Kenneth's sullen mood was a touchy subject. "I suppose he misses your mother."

Daisy narrowed her eyes. "We both do."

"I understand she married again. A Scot."

The burgundy gloves were tossed aside and Daisy flounced out of the shop. Clearly the Dowager Duchess' second marriage was another topic Daisy didn't want to discuss.

DAISY HAD BEEN DETERMINED to maintain her composure with Jasmine. They'd never been friends. She'd thrown

Jasmine at Payton King in the belief they were both gold-diggers. A crusty elderly relative accompanied the King brothers when they'd first come to London. Uncle Gregor let slip that the Kings had come to London in search of wealthy brides. The Foxworthys were in dire financial straits and it was common knowledge they hoped to marry off their daughter to a wealthy nobleman.

Daisy had plotted for Payton and Jasmine to fall in love then be heartbroken when they each discovered the other's motives. She'd done it because she thought herself in love with Payton and he with her.

She'd since realized it was his kilt and those powerful legs that fascinated her. Not only that, it turned out Payton and Jasmine planned to marry. Daisy would wager Jasmine's mother would do her upmost to undermine that possibility; what's more, she couldn't imagine Jasmine adapting to the wilds of Scotland. Nor did she understand what Payton saw in the witless chit. It was doubtful Jasmine would lower herself to work in the Kings' distillery, unlike Tavish's bride, Piper.

Daisy and her brother regularly received long letters from their mother. They described her new life in Glengeárr and how impressed she was with Piper's stalwart efforts to adapt to her new surroundings. She always included an invitation for Daisy and Kenneth to visit, and news about somebody called Cat. It was surprising there was ink left on the stationery after Kenneth read the letters over and over, but Daisy had no interest in traveling to Scotland and certainly didn't care about a woman with a ridiculous name like Cat.

And why was Jasmine asking after Kenneth? If only

Daisy understood the full reason her brother had withdrawn into himself. She suspected he'd met someone in Scotland—someone he didn't want to talk about. He never stopped singing their new stepfather's praises so she surmised Jock Graham wasn't the problem.

It was high time Daisy turned her brother's attention to thoughts of arranging a marriage for his sister. If Jasmine Foxworthy could get a man to the altar...

Worn out by the afternoon's shopping and the futile effort to take a liking to Daisy, Jasmine hoped to retreat to her bedroom before anyone knew she was home. It turned out to be a forlorn hope. "Was your shopping expedition a success?" her mother asked, appearing in the foyer before Bates had the front door closed.

"You're aware I don't have the funds to purchase anything," Jasmine replied. "I'm certain Lady Daisy Hawkins knows that. It's the reason she invited me to go shopping on London's most expensive street."

"You really must learn to be friends with the girl," her mother retorted. "It's the best way to get into the good graces of her brother."

"Mama, I've already told you I am not interested in the Duke of Ramsay. I have a beau."

"A penniless Scot," Lady Foxworthy exclaimed. "You can do so much better."

"Payton isn't penniless. His distillery makes money, and he says their whisky will make a lot more now the Regent's Royal Warrant..."

"Whisky! The very thought of my daughter marrying a man who brews a vile tasting beverage..."

"Please excuse me, Mama. I wish to lie down before dinner."

She took the stairs before her mother could object and breathed a sigh of relief when she entered her chamber.

She unlaced her half boots, toed them off and lay down on the bed fully clothed. Her lady's maid had been sent packing two years ago, so she didn't attempt to remove her day gown. Papa's gambling debts took precedence over wages.

The velvet drapes of her fourposter had been sold long ago, so she had an unobstructed view of the small room. Her gaze roamed over the familiar furnishings. The chintz curtains and matching quilt had faded; cheap reproductions of masterpieces adorned the walls; the top of the cedar chest was badly scratched. But she loved the cozy room where she'd slept since childhood.

Payton had spoken at length about his home in the Highlands. The house sounded rustic and Glengeárr remote. Jasmine had lived in London all her life. A bride expected to run her husband's household, but Tavish and Piper lived in the same house. She barely knew Piper and prayed she was friendlier than Daisy.

A future with Payton promised wealth, but the prospect of living in Scotland held no appeal. She really hadn't considered that when she'd first fallen for him. Surely he'd come to understand she couldn't leave London.

CATRIONA

"You don't seem quite yourself today, Your Grace," Mainwaring noted.

Kenneth's man of business was being polite. He hadn't *been himself* for months—not since his return from Scotland. He hadn't confided the reason to his own sister, so he wasn't about to tell Mainwaring he was pining for a woman. The man would think he'd lost his mind.

However, Mainwaring's remark was a sure sign he'd noticed Kenneth's lack of enthusiasm for his responsibilities. He'd thoroughly enjoyed his ducal duties—until he'd met Cat.

Life seemed meaningless without her. It was ludicrous. He'd barely spoken more than a dozen words to the raven-haired Scot, but she was in his soul. Her kiss of farewell said it all. She was as smitten with him as he was with her.

His mother had obviously noticed their attraction. Every letter was full of news of Catriona. But she was a lass born and bred in the Highlands, the granddaughter of a drayman. He'd felt at home in Glengeárr, but could never move to the remote glen from which his ancestors hailed. He'd discovered more of the Scot in him than he'd ever thought he possessed, but his duty lay in England.

Besides which, Cat's raven hair and dark eyes were more suited to a gypsy than a duchess.

"No," he said in response to Mainwaring's comment, wishing he hadn't conjured Cat's exotic features. "Scotland took more out of me than I expected."

"Of course," his employee agreed. "And you've had the added pressures of assisting with the *Uachdaran* venture now that you're back."

Little did Mainwaring know that working with Payton and Niven King to promote the distillery in which he and others had invested was the one arena where he found fulfillment. It was a link to Cat, his mother and the Highlands he'd left behind.

Catriona Neish poked at the peat fire in the hearth of her cottage. "I'm grateful to Piper King," she told her grandfather. "It was the English lass' influence with her husband that secured my employment at the *Uachdaran* distillery."

Seated in his favorite rocking chair and sucking on his pipe, he agreed. "Aye. Ye're the only lass allowed to assist with the distilling process itself when extra hands are needed."

Turning the malting barley by hand was hard work

and Cat was surprised Tavish had asked her to help. However, keeping the ledger up to date was her main responsibility. It was satisfying to see the profits mount.

"The fact ye've worked as a drayman for the King family for decades helped smooth the ruffled feathers of the predominantly male workforce."

A coughing fit delayed his reply. "Weel, yer wages are important now I'm too feeble to work," he wheezed.

It was true he seemed to have aged rapidly in the few months since the English investors came to inspect the distillery. It would be a lonely life when he passed on—a prospect she didn't want to think about.

"Ye're nay feeble," she retorted.

He made no reply, but she knew it hurt his pride to depend on her wages.

Generous investments by wealthy patrons, including Kenneth, and the Regent's granting of a Royal Warrant had changed the lives of everyone in the glen. Those windfalls had already doubled the business. More profits meant more employment for local people. For Cat there'd been another kind of change. Though they'd spent only brief moments together, she couldn't get Kenneth Hawkins, Duke of Ramsay, out of her head and her heart.

Her grandfather kept pestering to know the reason for her melancholy. How to tell him she'd foolishly fallen for an English duke?

It didn't help that she saw Kenneth's mother almost every day. The Dowager Duchess and her new husband were her neighbors. They had both invested in the distillery and enjoyed coming regularly to see how things were progressing. Lady Maureen talked about Kenneth constantly. He apparently spent most of his time planning the shipping and marketing of *Uachdaran* whisky with Payton and Niven King. She'd once thought she might marry Payton, but that was unlikely now. She didn't care that he was far away in London and apparently engaged to someone called Jasmine. Kenneth was the man she wanted—but couldn't have.

"Daisy writes that Kenneth is still despondent," Maureen, former Duchess of Ramsay, told her husband.

Jock chuckled. "Ye think he's pining for Catriona."

"Of course. You saw the way he looked at her when he was here. I know my son and I could tell he was drawn to her."

"Her grandfather told me she has changed and always seems preoccupied."

"She's smitten with my son."

"Maybe she's just concerned about all the new responsibilities Tavish has given her."

"No, I could tell as soon as they met there was something special between them. They are meant to be together."

He took her into his arms. "Just like us. I knew right off we were destined for each other."

"Aye. I kent it too, braw laddie," she quipped, imitating his brogue.

"I suppose neither o' them sees any future for a relationship," Jock said with a sigh.

Maureen nodded. "They probably think Kenneth can't marry a commoner. They've forgotten I was a commoner who married a wealthy Englishman who unexpectedly inherited a dukedom."

"Now, ye're my duchess," he whispered, nibbling her ear.

"I am," she agreed, melting into his solid body. "But we have to make both of them see I was no different from Cat when I ran away from Glengeárr with my Sassenach."

"I suspect ye've cooked up some scheme to accomplish that."

"Piper and I have been working on it."

PIPER GAZED at the month old babe who'd fallen asleep at her breast. Tiny as Munro was, she could see her husband's features already developing. "He'll grow to look like you," she whispered to Tavish.

He rose from the armchair in a corner of the bedroom and took his son. "Then I pity the bairn," he quipped, as he lay the babe in his cradle beside the bed.

Piper wasn't surprised he avoided looking at her bare breasts. They both longed for the day when they could do more than just pleasure each other with fingers and mouths. "Come to bed," she said seductively, confident his gaze would soon return to her still-bare breasts.

He lay down next to her, on top of the quilted coverlet and fully clothed.

"I need my naked Highlander to cuddle me," she coaxed, reaching for his hand.

He rolled on to his side and looked into her eyes. "We both ken we'll be tempted to do more than cuddle. How much longer?"

"Cat thinks two more weeks."

He sat up. "Ye discuss our lovemaking wi' Cat?"

"She's my only friend, and I don't feel comfortable asking your Aunty Maureen. The midwife's been called away to another village and who knows when she'll be back in Glengeárr. She wasn't very happy about helping deliver the babe of a Sassenach in any case."

Her complaints did the trick. Tavish stripped off his trews and shirt and joined her under the covers.

"You always feel warm," she said as she cuddled into his solid body.

"'Tis ye make me hot, Piper."

Smiling coyly, she came to her knees and swirled her tongue over the tip of his swollen manhood. "Not long now," she said before taking him into her mouth.

"Hasten the day," he growled. "Though I hope ye willna stop spoilin' me this way once I can bury myself inside ye again."

TAVISH GATHERED his wife into his arms after they'd pleasured each other. "I'm too selfish," he chuckled. "Ye've relieved my ache, though 'tis a waste o' good seed to come all o'er yer lovely breasts."

"Hush, you'll wake Munro and I want to sleep for a while before he demands to be fed again."

Tavish was content to spoon his body around Piper's back and cup a swollen breast. "I hope ye dinna tell Cat everything about us."

She nestled her warm bottom against his sated cock. "Of course not. That's private and precious to you and me. She wouldn't be interested in any case; she's too preoccupied with thoughts of Kenneth."

"Ye still think so, after all these months?"

"Yes. Kenneth writes to your Aunty Maureen about his work with Payton and Niven. Daisy's letters describe a moody, listless brother who refuses to talk about the woman he met in Scotland."

"And ye dinna think Cat is still pining for Payton?"

"Was she like this before when she was sweet on your brother?"

"Nay. That was just an adolescent crush. I agree she's changed."

"Well, your aunty and I are trying to think of a way to get them together."

"Good luck wi' that," he yawned as sleep claimed him.

VOLUNTEERS

Payton, Niven and Kenneth spent most days in the London offices of the Duke of Withenshawe's shipping empire, working to expand the whisky business.

When he lived in the Highlands, if anyone had asked Payton what he thought of the English nobility, he'd have been hard pressed not to swear in response. That was before he met Withenshawe and his own cousin, Kenneth. Both dukes had invested heavily in the King family's distillery in Glengeárr. Withenshawe had even offered free use of his shipping fleet for five years so the whisky could be transported by sea from Dundee to London.

But Payton had come to respect both men for the tireless efforts they'd put forth to establish a market for *Uachdaran* in England and even further afield. They were visibly frustrated by Napoleon's disruption of shipping routes, especially as far as Spain was concerned.

"Any news about the situation in Cádiz?" Payton asked the duke when he arrived.

"Nothing good," Withenshawe replied in answer to his question. "The siege continues. Could go on for months."

"It's been almost two years," Kenneth added.

"Sooner or later, Napoleon will be defeated," Niven suggested. "Then we can get our barrels. Tavish just has to be patient."

"I wish I shared your optimism, young man," Withenshawe replied. "The Little Emperor is greedy for power. He commands a vast, mighty army that has mowed down every country's army that's stood in his way. No city in Europe has ever withstood a siege by Bonaparte's forces."

"I agree," Payton declared. "We canna wait. I'll sail to Spain. Is there no other port we could use?"

"My captains tell me the safest port would be Gibraltar," Withenshawe replied. "British territory since 1713, it's more than fifty miles as the crow flies from your destination in Jerez. Beyond its borders, you'd have to cross dangerous terrain."

"Then I'll head for there, if ye can spare a ship and a crew, Yer Grace."

"'Tis too dangerous," Niven protested. "I dinna want to lose a brother for the sake of a few barrels."

"'Tisna about the barrels," Payton countered. "'Tis about Tavish's dream."

"The ship isn't a problem," Withenshawe said. "So long as you bring the crew back safely."

The dark humor brought a wry smile to every face, except Niven's.

"If ye're determined to go," Payton's little brother said. "Then I'm comin' with ye."

"No," Kenneth exclaimed. "We'd never hear the end of it from Uncle Gregor if anything happened to the two of you. I'll go with Payton."

KENNETH WAS ODDLY RELIEVED. He'd just volunteered to go to a war zone but felt no fear. He'd considered the possibility for a few days. Payton was bound and determined to retrieve the barrels, so why not go with him? It was preferable to wasting his life pining for what couldn't be. Perhaps he'd meet some sultry *señorita* who'd take his mind off Catriona.

Daisy wouldn't miss him. His mother didn't need to know until it was too late to do anything about it. As for Cat herself, well there was no future for them so what did it matter if he was killed?

But he was being too negative. He'd have to come back safely. He as yet had no heir to inherit as Duke of Ramsay. "How long to ready a ship, Withenshawe?" he asked.

"Ship's ready," came the reply. "A week to muster a suitable crew."

"Are ye sure ye want to sail to Spain?" Payton asked.

Kenneth detected a hint of hope in his cousin's question. "Aye," he quipped with a broad smile. "Somebody's got to keep an eye on ye."

"Glad 'tis ye," Payton replied, offering his hand.

Kenneth would once have refused the offer of a handshake from a commoner who failed to use his title when addressing him. Those pompous days were long gone. Payton didn't value his support as a duke, but as a comrade.

They both grimaced when Niven slammed the door on his way out.

"He'll come round," Payton assured him.

"I'll keep him busy looking for more warehouse space and finding new markets," Withenshawe said.

HIS GUT CHURNING with resentment and fear for his brother, Niven stood on the dock and looked out at the filthy Thames. He was sick and tired of being left out. Payton no longer consulted him about anything important. He was just as much a part of the *Uachdaran* distillery as anyone. Over the years, he'd spent hours hand turning the malt; he'd been up to his knees in bogs, cutting peat for the kilns; he'd harvested field after field of barley. Now, he was to be left behind twiddling his thumbs in a city he hated. Payton preferred to sail with their cousin than with his own brother.

Kenneth had been like a bear with a sore tooth since his return from Scotland. Now, he was visibly enthused about sailing to Spain with Payton. A man might think he was pining for a woman, but who could he have met in Glengeárr? Catriona Neish was the only attractive female and she...

"*Crivvens*," he exclaimed. "Kenneth and Cat?"

Should he mention his suspicions to Payton? Cat had once been sweet on his brother. Maybe she hadn't reciprocated Kenneth's feelings and therein lay the reason she hadn't come back to London with him.

A wave of homesickness suddenly washed over Niven. He might as well go home and help Tavish in the distillery. It would be a chance to see for himself if Cat was still pining for Payton. He'd have to tell her about Jasmine Foxworthy.

He obviously wasn't needed in London and there was a company ship leaving for Dundee in a few days.

A week later, Payton and Kenneth stood together on the deck of the *SS Matilda* as she glided along the Thames, headed for the open sea.

Jasmine hadn't come to see them off, but Payton hadn't expected her to. She was furious that he was leaving and couldn't believe he was off to war-torn Spain to retrieve a few barrels. "I'm going for Tavish," he'd explained, but she'd refused to listen.

In truth, he was looking forward to spending time apart. They'd have years together as man and wife. The prospect of taking her to the Highlands once they married made him shiver.

"Cold?" Kenneth asked.

"Aye," he lied, lest his cousin think him afraid. "I'm glad 'tis ye coming along."

If Niven had prevailed, Payton would have put all his energy into protecting his younger brother.

"We'll watch out for each other," Kenneth agreed.

ROUGH PASSAGE

Pounding her feather pillow, Jasmine fumed. Not only had Payton sailed away to Spain two days ago, he'd done so against her wishes. He'd told her he was sorry over and over, but that didn't lessen the betrayal. Evidently, a few wooden barrels were more important than she was. Surely they could make all the barrels they needed in Scotland? What sherry had to do with whisky was beyond her comprehension.

He'd promised they'd wed as soon as he returned. Did he expect her to cloister in her parents' home and live like a nun while he was gone? Who would escort her now? And what would become of her if the foolish man were killed?

Her long-suffering mother perched on the edge of the mattress. "It's a blessing, I tell you," she crowed for the umpteenth time.

"You're not helping matters, Mama," Jasmine retorted. "My heart is broken."

"Nonsense. Think on it. This is your opportunity to meet someone more suitable, someone who can rescue our finances. You're our only hope. It's your responsibility. Your father has already made enquiries among his card-playing friends. Do you really want to marry this Scot and traipse off to the wilds of Scotland? Ladies don't imbibe whisky, vile stuff that it is."

"But I love him," Jasmine wailed.

Lady Foxworthy rose with a sigh. "You'll soon get over him. I'll leave you now but your Papa and I expect you to dry those tears and come down for dinner."

Jasmine stared up at the ceiling after her mother left. Contrary to what her Mama believed, she hadn't shed a single tear over Payton's desertion. She admitted inwardly that she was more resentful than broken-hearted. Perhaps she didn't love him, but few people married for love. He was handsome and fun to be with. Seeing him in a kilt did funny things to her insides. Someday he'd be rich. That might have to be enough. Most eligible wealthy bachelors weren't interested in a girl from an impoverished family, especially gamblers who'd probably fleeced most of her father's money.

"THIS IS NAUGHT like sailing to Dundee," Payton shouted over the whine of the gale tossing the *SS Matilda* like a cork in the Cantabrian Sea.

"You've got that right," Kenneth replied, holding onto the slippery rail in the narrow companionway.

"After a week of this, it's a good thing neither us suffers from *mal de mer*."

"Aye. The captain warned us it wouldna be smooth sailin'."

"That was an understatement."

They'd gone up on deck to see if they could lend a hand, but the bosun demanded they return to the cabin they shared. The companionway was as far as they got and seemed a safer place to be if the ship went down.

"I thank ye for comin' wi' me on this perilous journey," Payton said.

"Seemed like a good idea at the time," Kenneth quipped.

Payton appreciated the irony. "Aye."

A short time later, Kenneth pressed a finger to his lips. "Am I imagining it or has the wind lessened?"

"We're still tossin' but mayhap nay as much," Payton agreed.

"It'll be calmer now," a sailor confirmed as he shuffled by and removed his oilskins. "We'll be sailing by Portugal soon."

"Where Napoleon holds sway," Kenneth remarked.

"True," the sailor sniffled as water dripped from his hair. "But the coast is mostly quiet. Different story when we reach the Bay of Cádiz and the narrow Strait of Gibraltar. Captain Frame will likely take us through at night when it's dark. What Frenchie can't see, he can't hit. Even when he can see, he often misses!"

Chuckling, the sailor moved on, dripping water the length of the companionway.

Having sailed by the Portuguese coast without incident, Kenneth and Payton were summoned to the captain's cabin the next afternoon.

"We'll be dropping anchor soon," Frame explained. "We're far enough out in the Bay of Cádiz to be beyond the range of French artillery. That might not hold true once we make for the strait."

"How wide is it?" Kenneth asked.

"About eight miles at the narrowest point between Spain and Morocco," Frame replied. "We'll wait out in the bay and sail through at night in the hope British guns will come to our rescue if the French open fire from Spain."

"Do we ken if the French have taken up positions overlooking the strait?" Payton asked.

"Hard to say. They're still trying to capture Cádiz, so I expect most of their artillery is concentrated there. It's well known the French army is being harassed by armed partisans—local people who seem to be doing a better job than the Spanish army. Spaniards responded to the defeats suffered by their army by continuing the fight on their own. No country in Europe was less prepared than Spain to defeat Bonaparte. The state was bankrupt, the king and his government hated by the people. Yet, the partisans are thwarting the Emperor's plans. He must be furious!"

"How are they managing that?" Kenneth asked.

"Laying deadly ambushes, disrupting supply lines, stealing weapons and ammunition, killing soldiers, and so on. They strike then disappear and they know the terrain much better than the French. It's a new way of waging war. Gone are the days when opposing sides invited each other to fire first as they reportedly did at Fontenoy in 1745. In Spain, priests, women and children plot the murder of isolated soldiers. They are willing to suffer any hardship to recover their independence. You're more likely to run into them and not Napoleon's soldiers on your trek to Jerez."

"Let's hope these partisans dinna shoot before asking questions," Payton opined.

"The British have been helping them. There's probably somebody in Gibraltar who can guide you to them."

~

Payton and Kenneth were allowed to remain on deck during the passage through the Strait of Gibraltar. They couldn't see much in the pitch-black of night—just the vague dark outline of land on either side.

"Frame thinks this schooner is too small to be of concern to the French," Kenneth whispered.

"Let's hope he's right," Payton replied.

"Too bad we're passing through the Pillars of Hercules in the dark," Kenneth said. "I'd love to have seen the sight."

"Is that what they're called?" Payton asked.

"In ancient times. Phoenicians, Romans and other traders came his way."

Payton pondered this new knowledge. The lands on either side of the strait—Africa on one side, Europe on the other—had stood as silent witnesses to the passing of untold thousands of ships.

He was jolted from his musings when a cheer went up. The crew had sighted the lights of Gibraltar ahead. Now, the real adventure would begin.

PARTISANS
SIERRA MORENA, ANDALUCÍA, SOUTHERN SPAIN

María Alba worried about her father. Anger and hatred had consumed Pedro Castillero since his wife's rape and murder by Napoleon's soldiers. He blamed himself for not protecting his beloved. Alba had lived a peaceful, happy life with her Spanish father and Scottish mother—until the French invaded Spain four years ago.

At first, Napoleon seemed content to overrun large towns in the north, but then he'd taken Madrid, removed the king and installed his own brother in his place. The Castilleros and their fellow countrymen were incensed. They might not love Charles IV but he was *their* king. It was for Spaniards to decide if he should abdicate—and a Frenchman could *not* be King of Spain.

Napoleon's army was now on the march through the south. They'd captured Sevilla and spent almost two years besieging the strategic port of Cádiz. Located on the supply route between French headquarters in Sevilla and the besieged port, the Castillero sherry *bodega* in Jerez stood in their path. Alba never understood the reason for the destruction of a harmless *bodega*. During the vicious attack, the precious fortified wine was consumed or poured out on the cobblestones to mingle with the blood of innocent peasants. Anything the invaders could lay their greedy hands on was smashed. The *bodega* and the vines were put to the torch.

Forewarned of the attack, Alba and her parents fled to a nearby village, but French soldiers came a day later and took away the women. Alba hid in a hayloft, otherwise she'd have disappeared with her mother. Days later, Olivia Castillero's ravished body was found in a ditch, along with many others. They'd all had their throats cut.

Until then, the war had been a far-off thing. Now, it was real. Alba and her father joined the thousands of outraged Spaniards who waged war against the invaders. They became part of the hidden people's army that harassed the French rearguard, cutting off supply lines and laying ambushes. Napoleon knew how to win on the battlefield, but seemed to have no strategy against an unseen enemy. The French feared and hated the *guerrillas* and reprisals were common. The partisans exacted brutal revenge for every atrocity. Alba had quickly learned to kill without feeling remorse.

"Do you remember the songs Mama taught me?" she asked her father one night in an effort to take his mind off the awful memories and the dangers they faced.

He continued to stare into the flames of the campfire, seemingly oblivious to her presence and the dozen or so comrades sleeping on the ground nearby.

He finally raised his head when she began to croon a Gaelic lament. "You look just like her," he whispered.

"I miss her too, Papa, but we're avenging her suffering and death every day."

"Hiding in the forests of the Sierra is no life for a beautiful young girl," he countered hoarsely, his eyes filled with tears.

She reached for his calloused hand. "It's a long time since I even looked like a girl, and this is the right life for any Spaniard who cares about our liberty and our country," she retorted. "But anger makes you careless when we attack. I don't want to be alone, Papa."

"I'll be more cautious," he promised.

But he couldn't meet her gaze and she had to accept that he longed to be reunited with her dead mother.

"If I lose you, there'd be nothing left to live for," she lied. She'd fight for a Spain free of the French until her dying breath.

Rustling noises in the bushes brought every man in the camp to his feet, weapon in hand.

"*Amigo*, ho," came the shout recognized as the British spy who brought supplies and intelligence about developments in the war.

They suspected John Smith wasn't his real name, but they were always glad to see him and recognized he took enormous risks on their behalf. Of course, Alba wasn't naive enough to believe the British didn't have a vested interest in ridding Spain of Napoleon. The Spanish army wasn't large or strong enough to accomplish a total victory even if they won the occasional battle. According to John, Alba's little band and thousands like it all across

Spain were making a difference. His encouraging words kept hope alive.

"What news?" was on everyone's lips.

John cocked his head toward the mule. "I brought more English rifles."

Several men set about relieving the animal of its precious burden. Bonaparte's troops favored the Charleville musket, a weapon that dated back to the French Revolution. A modern invention, the rifles were considered to be more accurate.

"Also, two men are due to land in Gibraltar any day," John told them as he claimed a spot by the campfire. "They wish to go to Jerez."

"Why?" Alba's father asked.

"I don't know any more than what I've told you. They're coming from London, so I assume they are English."

"My father and I both speak their language," Alba said. "And you are aware we are from Jerez. We can guide them."

Always the naysayer, Alfonso Rodriguez shook his head. "But you don't know the reason for their journey."

"It must be important if they're willing to risk their lives for it," Alba's father replied gruffly. "Bring them to us."

Alba lay awake for a long time that warm night, gazing up at the canopy of stars. Her Scottish mother had been gifted with the sight. She'd warned of the attack on the *bodega*. Had Olivia Castillero foreseen the manner of her own death? For reasons she didn't understand, Alba sensed the arrival of the mysterious Englishmen would change her life forever. Their willingness to risk their lives to travel to Jerez was curious. The town had no other claim to fame besides its sherry *bodegas*.

Returning to Jerez would dredge up terrible memories of death and destruction. But she'd known many happy years growing up there, so perhaps there was a reason Fate was leading her back to the place of her birth.

JOHN SMITH

"It's like being back in England," Kenneth said as he and Payton strolled along the narrow streets of Gibraltar. "Apart from the great rock looming over the town."

"We're used to mountains in Scotland," Payton replied. "But nay this humid weather."

"Aye."

Payton chuckled. "Ye sound more like a Scot every day since ye came back from Glengeárr."

"Scotland changed me," Kenneth admitted.

Payton had certainly noticed a change in his cousin's demeanor, but hadn't wanted to pry. But here they were, the two of them, poised to undertake a perilous journey together. They'd got through the risky voyage and navigated the Strait unscathed but…

"Niven thinks ye're pining for a lass."

Kenneth stopped abruptly and stared up at the Rock.

Payton expected to be told to mind his own business,

but his cousin looked him in the eye and said, "He's right."

"Do ye want to tell me who it is?"

"You might call me out if I do."

Payton searched his memory. Kenneth was apparently enamored of a lass he thought Payton cared for. There was only one. "Ye dinna mean Catriona Neish?"

"Aye," Kenneth rasped.

"Wheest, man, I was a young lad in love wi' every lass, though I admit I cared for Cat. She's a good person."

"I can't get her out of my thoughts."

"Do ye think she cares for ye?"

"Mother tells me in her letters that Cat admitted as much to Piper."

"Then why did ye nay bring her back to London?"

Kenneth shook his head. "I'm a duke. A commoner from the Highlands can't be a duchess."

"And yet, yer Mam was a commoner who hailed from Glengeárr, and she became a duchess."

"That was different. My father never expected to inherit a dukedom."

"But he did."

~

KENNETH PONDERED his cousin's words as they walked back to the Governor's mansion where they'd been billeted. The British Governor seemingly couldn't do enough for his titled guest and Kenneth enjoyed the preferential treatment.

But the deference raised a question in his mind. Had

he been too much of a snob to realize Cat *could* be his duchess? His own mother would certainly help her adjust to that life. He had a feeling Maureen Hawkins-Graham was already plotting something of the sort.

Standing stock still in the foyer, he was suddenly filled with an urge to rush back aboard ship and return to Scotland…or he could write to his mother and ask her to bring Cat to London…or…

"Kenny Hawkins, is that you?"

It had been a long while since anyone had called him Kenny, not since…

"Jim Beatty?" he asked, scarcely believing he'd come face to face with a chum from his days at Eton and Oxford.

Jim touched a finger to his lips. "Yes, it's me, but here I'm John Smith."

Kenneth was aware Jim had joined the British army after university and been involved in some hush-hush maneuvers. He must have a good reason for using a false name. "John Smith, I'd like to introduce you to my cousin, Payton King."

The two men shook hands.

"This old pal and I helped each other survive Eton," Kenneth explained.

John stared at Payton's tartan trews. "I take it you're a Scot. That outfit will have to go, I'm afraid. And Kenny, you look much too gentrified to be a Spanish peasant."

"I'm nay understandin'" Payton said.

"I'll guide you to a group of partisans and you'll have to look like peasants if you want to be accepted. It's up to them to get you the rest of the way to Jerez."

"We couldn't be in better hands," Kenneth said.

"But I warn you," Smith cautioned. "The partisans are a hardened lot. War has turned ordinary people into killers. They'll only help you if they believe your mission is important to their cause."

"Weel," Payton replied. "Our mission, as ye put it, is to retrieve our barrels."

"Barrels?"

"Aye. My brothers and I operate a distillery in the Highlands. Some time ago, we shipped staves to Spain so they could be made into barrels and filled with sherry. The arrangement was always that we'd get them back after a few years."

Smith shook his head. "That sounds ridiculous. You're risking your lives for this? What will you do with empty barrels?"

"Age our single malt whisky in them."

"Whisky?"

"Aye. *Uachdaran*. Mayhap ye've heard o' it?"

"As it happens, I have. Bloody good whisky." He tapped his chin for a few minutes, then said, "One of the partisans used to operate a sherry distillery in Jerez. It might not sound like a fool's errand to him."

~

THE NEXT DAY, clad in what could only be described as third-hand clothing, Payton and Kenneth mounted mules and followed John Smith out of Gibraltar, headed north. At home in Scotland, Payton had no need of a mount. Kenneth's grimace left no doubt that he'd never ridden such a lowly beast.

John armed them with pistols. A pack animal carried a cache of weapons and other supplies.

For three days, they made slow progress through rugged terrain. The heat was oppressive. The extra mule often stubbornly objected to its burden and refused to go any further. Payton eventually learned to coax his own temperamental animal to obey his commands, but that didn't lessen the discomfort in his rear end. His outfit hadn't smelled too sweet when they first set out. The borrowed boots were tight and the soles well worn. They washed their hands and faces in mountain streams, but it was too risky to disrobe completely. Payton longed to be clean again.

John told them more about the partisans. "They've forced the French to deploy thousands of troops to provide escort for the delivery of supplies."

"Sounds like their tactics are successful," Kenneth replied. "An invisible army."

"Yes," John agreed. "Although, sometimes they fight shoulder to shoulder with the Spanish army."

John assured them the French rarely ventured into the sierras for fear of encountering *guerillas*. "They have instilled fear in the hearts of enemy soldiers and that's a powerful weapon."

Kenneth nodded. "Indeed. Napoleon's troops have always considered themselves invincible."

"Well, they're getting more demoralized by the day here in Spain. Desertion is becoming common, despite the risk of execution."

Payton deemed it a tragedy that such a beautiful country should be torn apart by war. "Reminds me o' campin' out in the Cairngorms," he whispered to his cousin on the third night sleeping under the stars.

The howl of a wolf shattered the silence.

"Wolves an' all," he added.

"They'll not venture near the fire," John said.

"Still, I'll keep my pistol to hand," Kenneth replied. "How much further till we find these partisans?"

"Not far," John replied. "Actually, they'll find us."

RESTLESS

In London, as one long day followed another, Lady Daisy Hawkins grew more restless. With Kenneth gone off to Spain, Ramsay House seemed even more empty than usual. Mainwaring came and went occasionally but Kenneth's man of business rarely exchanged more than a few polite pleasantries with his employer's sister.

Niven King was the only other occupant of the house. He left early every morning to work with the Duke of Withenshawe's people in the company offices near the London docks. He came home late in the evening and went directly to his room.

Her Scottish cousin had been moody ever since Payton's departure. Evidently, he didn't approve of his brother's Spanish adventure any more than Daisy approved of Kenneth's decision to go with him.

It was her brother's responsibility to arrange a marriage for her. He should be escorting her to balls and musicales, not haring off to war-torn Spain.

Daisy fervently wished she'd never heard of *Uachdaran* whisky.

Her mother's letters didn't help. They were full of excited news about the mounting profits of the King distillery, and the mysterious Cat person. Her mother was obviously happy in Scotland with her new husband, so Daisy didn't have the heart to tell her that Kenneth had gone off to war.

She ought to enquire after Payton's fiancée, but preferred her own company to that of Jasmine Foxworthy. As the only person served by a battery of servants in the enormous dining room, she felt lonely and ridiculous but couldn't imagine making small talk with Jasmine over dinner.

It was enough to make her contemplate the unthinkable—a trek to Scotland.

~

Niven was restless. Aided by the Duke of Withenshawe's staff, he'd found a large, secure warehouse not far from the dock used by the duke's ships. It was a major step forward. To date, Tavish had shipped sufficient product to meet demands. Now, they could pursue new markets, confident they had extra stock on hand. The barrels aging in the cellar for five years or more could be tapped.

If Payton hadn't gone to Spain, Niven could have shared this small triumph with him. Instead, he had to content himself with congratulatory slaps on the back from the duke's men.

He'd put off sailing to Scotland when negotiations

looked like they might prove fruitful. Here in London, there was only Daisy left to tell, and she wouldn't understand or care about the importance of the warehouse. Why not sail home and tell Tavish in person? His elder brother would appreciate his achievement.

Resolved to inform Daisy of his imminent departure, he left the offices early. Upon his arrival at Ramsay House, he informed Harrison he'd be home for dinner.

"Lady Daisy will be pleased," the butler replied.

Doubting the veracity of that statement, Niven took the stairs to his room. He packed his few belongings and decided to don his kilt for his last meal at Ramsay House.

∾

INFORMED that Niven King would be at home for dinner, Daisy arrived in the dining room early. It was silly to be excited, but she was tired of eating alone. Niven wasn't as good a conversationalist as Payton, but he was a pleasant enough fellow. At least there'd be some interaction with another human being, even if the conversation were only about the confounded whisky venture. Niven must be accomplishing something at the offices he went off to every day.

She probably should take more interest. Kenneth and their mother had invested heavily in *Uachdaran*. Who would have thought that the very proper Dowager Duchess Maureen Hawkins would spend her days eagerly visiting her nephews' distillery?

Daisy simply didn't understand the appeal of Scotland. The blessed country her mother had left thirty years ago had enthralled her when she'd gone back. Kenneth hadn't been the same since his visit. He even spoke with a noticeable brogue these days. Perhaps he'd spent too much time with his Highlander cousins. Goodness knows what he'd be like when he came back from spending weeks in Spain with Payton. *If* he came back...

"Cheer up," Niven said as he entered the dining room.

Daisy gaped. He'd worn his kilt and plaid. She had never noticed how tall he was, how broad-shouldered. "You're..."

"Aye, yer cousin, Niven," he chuckled as he took his seat. " I ken I dinna eat here verra often, but surely ye recognize me?"

His deep voice thrummed through her. Her throat suddenly felt as dry as the desert. "I...I..."

"Are ye nay feelin' well?' he asked.

Daisy swallowed hard. This was ridiculous. She'd barely paid attention to the youngest of her cousins and now she was salivating over him. "I'm perfectly fine," she replied, hoping he didn't detect the hoarseness in her voice.

"Sounds like ye might have a touch o' laryngitis," he said, sipping a spoonful of soup. "Several men at the shipyards have come down wi' it."

Laryngitis wasn't her problem. Inexplicable lust was. "Speaking of whisky," she heard herself say. "How are things going with our investment?"

∼

Niven wondered what game Daisy was playing. Once upon a time, she'd toyed with Payton then tossed him away. Perhaps now it was his turn. Tavish once said Daisy had a thing for kilts. Perhaps that was it. "Aye. Everyone involved will be glad to hear I've leased a secure warehouse that's more than big enough, for now."

"Excellent," she gushed. "You must be pleased with yourself."

"Ye've barely touched yer soup," he remarked, wondering what had become of the sullen Daisy. She was actually very attractive when she smiled.

"I'm not hungry," she replied. "It's simply good to have someone to converse with over dinner."

So, that explained her friendly demeanor. Her eyes were so wide, he could see they were a warm brown—something he'd never noticed before. Perhaps he should have come home for dinner more often. They'd hardly spoken during the past weeks which was rather silly considering they were the only two people living in the house. But he'd be gone on the morrow. "By the by," he said, strangely reluctant to tell her. "I've arranged passage on one of the ships going to Dundee."

Her broad smile fled. For one terrible moment, he feared she might burst into tears. "I'm homesick," he confessed. "I miss my brothers."

"Of course," she replied hoarsely. "I understand. I miss Kenneth. When are you leaving?"

"Tomorrow."

She stared at the uneaten food placed before her by the footman. "Gosh, we're just getting to know each other."

Niven hardly thought one dinner constituted getting to know each other. They'd met months ago. Still, they might have become friends if...

"Will you play the fiddle for me again before you go?" she asked.

Niven hadn't played since the night of the ball organized to welcome the Kings to London. A group of them had demonstrated a reel. "Now?"

"James can get the instrument from the music room."

The footman nodded and left.

Daisy poked at her food while they waited. She seemed uncharacteristically nervous. He felt a wee bit off balance himself. Still, the music would settle his nerves.

"I didn't want Kenneth to go to Spain," she confessed so softly he almost didn't hear.

"I was furious wi' Payton," he replied. "Still am."

"What will we do if they don't come back?"

Niven didn't even want to consider the possibility of losing a brother. However, if Kenneth lost his life there'd be a problem with the succession. Daisy could lose everything. No wonder she'd been sullen the last little while. He swallowed the lump in his throat when James arrived with the ancient violin. He tuned up the instrument, got to his feet and launched into his favorite reel.

Daisy tapped her feet for a while. Then she started to beat the rhythm on the table with both hands. It wasn't long before she stood and began to move back and forth in time to the music. Before he knew it, they were dancing an impromptu reel together though he played on, the music taking hold of him as it always did.

Finally, he stopped and they collapsed into their respective chairs, both laughing breathlessly.

Appealingly red in the face, bosom heaving, Daisy suddenly burst into tears and wailed, "I'm coming with you to Scotland."

Niven didn't think that was such a good idea if she was coming down with laryngitis, but it might help pass the time if she came with him. After all, she must miss her mother. "I'll see to it," he said.

FLIRTATION

Using hand signals, Alba's father called a halt in a grove of hawthorn bushes. Locating John Smith and his traveling companions hadn't taken much effort. There was a limited number of mountain trails John could take from Gibraltar. The band remained hidden for a while, listening to the foreigners' whispered conversations. Smith had said the visitors were English. One of them definitely was, but Alba felt sure the other man was a Scot. His brogue reminded her of her darling mother. Swallowing the regret in her throat, she followed her father and his comrades into the clearing.

Two men whirled to face them, pistols drawn. One was tall; the other a head taller.

"Put your weapons away," John advised, still hunkered down by the campfire. "They are friends."

The two lowered the pistols.

"These are the gentlemen I told you about," John informed Alba's father.

The giant stepped forward and offered his hand. "An honor to meet ye. I'm..."

Her father accepted the handshake, but interrupted the newcomer. "No names," he declared, holding up his hand. "Safer that way. We are all called Juan."

The foreigner had spoken only a word or two but Alba recognized the brogue. She also couldn't ignore the dizzying wave of lust that swept over her. He was tall, well-muscled and handsome, but so was the other man and countless others she'd met since the beginning of the war. Was it simply because he might be a Scot that she was drawn to him? Her mother had told her tales of the Highlands. She'd bestowed the ancient name of her country on her daughter. Alba had never set foot in Scotland, but that faraway land was part of her. She suddenly longed to know the stranger's name, but such knowledge could prove dangerous if either of them fell into enemy hands.

Her father's voice jolted her back to the glade. "Barrels?" he exclaimed. "For whisky?"

Surely, it couldn't be? However, as the exchange of information continued, it became clear the foreigners had come to retrieve the barrels Pedro Castillero had agreed years ago to return to Scotland. Venturing back to their ruined *bodega* would expose them to extreme danger, but her father had given his word. His honor would compel him to help the Scot and his companion fulfill their mission.

~

PAYTON AND THE PASSIONATE PARTISAN

Payton found himself at a loss—a rare occurrence for him. The guerrilla band's leader had said his name was Juan and that all his comrades were called Juan. It was reminiscent of the ubiquitous Jacques adopted by the revolutionaries in France. Keeping true names hidden ensured anonymity and protection.

But if all the partisans were indeed men, Payton was in trouble. The slight figure who'd stood close to the leader throughout the exchange was dressed in male clothing but had to be a woman. Why else had his manhood stirred?

And therein lay an even more puzzling dilemma. Payton was drawn to big-breasted women, not twig-like, mucky-faced waifs who looked about sixteen years old. However, he understood why a lass involved in guerrilla activities would want to dress and act like a man. He wished he could ask her name, just to be sure she was a lass. She probably didn't understand English, though her leader spoke it well enough. Was he her father?

It became obvious in the course of the conversation that this was the man who'd operated a vineyard in Jerez. He declared himself willing to lead them there. His comrades seemed less willing, reluctant even.

Despite the grumbling, it was agreed they would set off at dawn.

"What are the chances this Juan is the Spaniard you consigned the barrel staves to?" Kenneth asked as he and Payton bedded down for the night.

"Highly unlikely," he replied, though he wondered.

Alba was used to sleeping lightly. She wasn't surprised when many of her comrades drifted away during the night, probably encouraged to defect by Alfonso. Had the foreigners been aware of their defection? She was too far away to see if they were asleep, but the Scot was restless. Hopefully, he hadn't guessed she was a female, though she somehow doubted it. She'd seen lust in men's eyes before. It normally raised her hackles and her guard. What was different about the Scot? She'd preened under his gaze.

Opening her eyes to the pre-dawn darkness, she startled to see a man looming over her. Such carelessness could mean death, and how had the giant managed to move so stealthily?

"Good morn," he said, offering his hand. "Do ye speak English?"

Ignoring his offer of assistance, she came to her knees and rolled up the furs. "I do," she replied, swallowing the instinct to reply with *Aye*.

"Am I to call ye Juana, then?" he asked, a hint of amusement in his voice.

He was flirting with her. The powerful urge to reveal her real name had to be stifled, as did the temptation to be equally flirtatious. "If you wish," she replied coolly.

"Is the leader yer father?"

Alba saw no benefit in denying it. "He is."

"And he used to operate a sherry distillery in Jerez?"

The bittersweet memories clogged her throat. "The French destroyed it. And we call it a *bodega*."

"My brothers and I own a whisky distillery in Scotland. Been in our family for generations. I canna imagine how I'd feel if it were destroyed."

She could only nod in reply lest the tears start to fall. She'd buried the nightmare. The Scot had resurrected it.

"How is it ye speak such good English?" he asked.

Was there danger in telling him? "My mother was from the Isle of Mull," she confessed.

~

PAYTON LONGED to put his arms around this young lass who'd suffered great losses and was living the dangerous life of a guerrilla. Despite the ragged clothing and disheveled appearance, there was a quiet dignity about her. He had to assume her mother was dead since she obviously wasn't traveling with the partisans. But Scottish blood ran in her daughter's veins!

Her father appeared and shouldered him aside. "*Por favor*, stay away from my daughter, *Señor*," he warned.

Payton didn't blame him. Spaniards were notoriously protective of daughters—a difficult task at the best of times, which these weren't. "O' course," he replied. "I meant no disrespect."

The man was right. There was no point flirting with the Spanish lass. Eventually, he'd be sailing back to England. Jasmine was waiting anxiously for his return. The prospect held little joy.

He rejoined Kenneth who was busy saddling his mule.

"Tempting," his cousin said, cocking his head in Alba's direction.

"Nay," he lied.

~

In England, Kenneth had never saddled his own mount. Even before his father became a duke, the Hawkins family had employed grooms to take care of such menial tasks. Now, he was an expert at saddling a stubborn mule.

Coming along on this adventure had been a good idea. He still missed Cat, but there were other things to think about besides his deep yearning for a woman who seemed farther away than ever.

He hadn't fully appreciated the danger until they'd met up with the partisans—ordinary people who'd given up everything to hide in forests and harass the French. If he and his cousin were to survive, they'd have to keep their wits about them. It was obvious the diminutive Spanish woman had snagged Payton's attention. That in itself was intriguing. Well-endowed females were Payton's cup of tea. "Don't forget, Jasmine's waiting for you," he cautioned as they mounted. "And we need to keep our minds on the mission."

"Understood," came the half-hearted reply.

An Unlikely Trio

Niven had assumed he wouldn't see much of Daisy during the voyage north. However, it was difficult to avoid the only other passenger on the small schooner.

At first, he thought it merely inevitable they run into each other, but he soon realized Daisy was going out of her way to bump into him. And the meetings always seemed to occur in confined spaces, like the companionways, or the galley, where two people had to cram into a bench designed for one.

Strangely, he found himself looking forward to these encounters that involved somewhat inappropriate touching. His manhood definitely approved of the physical contact. He also discovered she was unexpectedly good company and a lively conversationalist.

She'd always seemed cool to the notion of traveling to Scotland and he wondered what had changed her mind.

She asked him all manner of questions about

Glengeárr and the distillery. It was evident she was nervous about the adventure, so he did his best to reassure her. "'Tis true life in the Highlands is different from what ye're used to in London. Simpler. Slower."

"I hope Mama won't mind my coming without letting her know," she said. "She's invited me more than once."

"I'm sure she'll be thrilled," he replied. He didn't know his Aunty Maureen all that well, but she'd always struck him as a loving parent.

"I'm anxious to meet this Cat person Mama writes about."

"She's a great lass," Niven replied, wondering if Daisy had put two and two together and realized it was Cat that Kenneth missed.

~

DAISY TOLD herself over and over that her pursuit of Niven King was foolhardy. She'd hardly noticed him for months; now, she couldn't go five minutes without becoming restless to see him again.

It was too bad he hadn't worn his kilt, though it probably wasn't an appropriate garment for a sea voyage. She wished she could wear something other than ankle length skirts that were an embarrassing nuisance to control in the wind.

Even covered in trews, the solid strength of his thigh was exciting when they sat side by side in the galley. She couldn't imagine why he would be nervous and soon got used to the constant twitching of his leg. A man thing, she supposed. It only got worse on the one occasion she plucked up her courage and put a hand on his knee to still the twitching.

He behaved like a perfect gentleman. Had she not dropped enough hints and carried on like a wanton? By the time they docked in Dundee, she feared she might have to simply kiss him first.

She stood on the deck, watching him supervise the unloading of the staves made of English oak that Tavish had asked for. A wagon pulled up beside the piles of staves. The grinning driver jumped down and embraced Niven. Daisy's curiosity turned to jealous anger when she realized the driver was a gypsy woman clad in men's overalls.

~

"I'm home," was the only thought in Niven's head as Catriona Neish embraced him, laughter bubbling from her throat.

"'Tis good to see ye," she gushed, thumping him on the back.

"Good to be home and to see yer bonnie face," he replied, dreading the moment he'd have to tell her about Kenneth.

That thought reminded him that Daisy was still on deck. He looked up and waved. She seemed angry for some reason. He cupped his hands to his mouth and shouted, "Come and meet Cat."

He was relieved when her smile returned and she headed for the gangway.

"Who is she?" Cat teased with a glint in her eyes. "Yer lady-love?"

The question took Niven aback. He liked Daisy, but she could hardly be called his lady-love. She'd traveled to Scotland to see her mother not to be with him. "Nay. Daisy is Kenneth's sister."

Cat studied her feet. "And how is he?"

"Kenneth? Weel..."

"Tell me," she demanded, eyes wide.

Clearly, she'd detected his hesitation. "I dinna ken how to tell ye."

"My brother's gone off to Spain," Daisy declared as she joined them on the dock.

Niven could cheerfully have strangled Daisy in that moment, but at least he'd been spared.

"Spain?" Cat rasped.

"Aye. He and Payton..."

"Payton has gone to Spain with him?"

"Aye."

Cat had always been the most level-headed, calm person he knew. Now, she shook alarmingly, chin quivering, fists clenched. "Kenneth," she wailed as the tears fell.

"You're the one," Daisy said softly, taking Cat's hand. "It's you my brother's been pining for."

∽

CAT STRUGGLED to calm the turmoil raging in her heart. Lady Maureen had hinted that Kenneth missed her, but she hadn't really believed it. "I came to Dundee to take delivery of these barrel staves," she explained when Niven had finished loading them onto the wagon.

"But why has yer Da nay come?" Niven asked.

"He canna work now. Too old, and the distillery's so busy, Tavish couldna spare a worker."

She longed to find the right words to say to Kenneth's sister, an Englishwoman she'd never met and who likely thought Cat a trollop angling to ensnare a duke. She wished she wasn't dressed in men's overalls. "I wasna expectin' passengers," she finally said. "I planned to sleep in the wagon tonight, but we can stop at an inn on the way."

"Aye," Niven replied. "Probably best."

Lady Daisy said nothing, her gaze fixed on the wagon.

"Dinna fash," Niven told her. "I'll ride in the back with the staves."

Cat didn't relish the prospect of sitting beside Kenneth's sister for hours on end. "Nay. We can fit three on the driver's seat."

"In that case, I'll take the reins," he replied.

Squeezed together, Niven seated between Cat and Lady Daisy, the three set off for Glengeárr.

After a few miles, Cat noticed the Englishwoman link her arm in Niven's. "I'm afraid of falling off," she said.

Cat had never seen Niven blush before. He might not think Daisy Hawkins was his lady-love. She obviously saw things differently. "Yer mother will be so pleased to see ye, Lady Daisy," she tried. Somebody had to start a conversation. They couldn't travel all the way to Glengeárr in total silence.

"I've missed her," came the unexpectedly candid reply.

"She misses ye, as well."

"Do you see her often?"

"Every day."

"Her letters are full of news of you, Catriona."

This came as a surprise. "Really?"

"Of course, that isn't for my benefit. It's for Kenneth's, isn't it? He reads them over and over."

Cat could summon no response, so she kept silent.

"Why didn't you travel to London with him?"

"He didn't ask me."

"Because he's a fool."

WHAT'S IN A NAME?

Payton had been warned off by a protective Spanish father. It wasn't hard to heed that warning during the day. Narrow mountain trails, a cantankerous mule, and the ever-present danger of running into a French patrol made it relatively easy to keep his mind off the young Spanish lass with whom he traveled.

The evening was a different proposition. With only Juan, his daughter, Payton and Kenneth sitting around a campfire, it seemed ludicrous not to engage in conversation. He wanted to know more about the resourceful lass who intrigued him. It was she who trapped and skinned the rabbits her father cooked over the open fire.

"Ye've adapted to this life," he said, instantly regretting the thoughtless words.

Juan clenched his fists. Even Kenneth grimaced.

"We've had to adapt," the lass replied. "Our old life is gone."

Payton detected no rancor in her reply, so he soldiered on. "Tell me about life before the French came."

The tears welling in her eyes proved he'd erred again. Juan spoke before he could apologize. "When we reach my *bodega*, you will see only destruction. Buildings and vines put to the torch."

"And our beautiful house," Juana added, her jaw clenched. "But that wasn't our biggest loss."

Father and daughter stared into the crackling flames.

Payton knew in that terrible moment that someone dear to them had died at the hands of the French soldiers. "Your mother?" he asked softly.

Struggling to hold on to her composure, Juana nodded. "*Sí, mi madre.*"

Payton's mother had been married to a man she despised. It had turned her into a shrew who often took out her resentment on her three sons. Nevertheless, her death left him feeling bereft. "I'm sorry," seemed an inadequate response to the Spaniards' obvious grief.

"What about the *bodega* where the Kings sent the barrel staves?" Kenneth asked. "Castillero was the man's name. Do you know him?"

"*Sí*," Juan replied. "I know him."

Payton and Kenneth exchanged a knowing glance. They'd both detected the truth in Juan's eyes. He was Pedro Castillero, the Spaniard to whom the Kings had consigned the staves.

In that case, there perhaps wasn't much hope of finding barrels intact if his *bodega* had been destroyed. Were these Spaniards leading them on a wild goose chase? If so, why?

Payton decided to take a more circuitous route to uncover the truth. "Ye said yer Ma was from Mull. How did yer parents meet?"

～

Alba was immensely proud of the familiar tale she hadn't been able to tell for years. Why not share something of her family's history with this intriguing Scot and his cousin? It was clear they were honorable men who would not betray confidences. The Castillero *bodega* had benefited from the excellent quality barrels from Scotland, shipped to them at no charge with only her father's word as guarantee of their return. No one could have predicted that Napoleon would put paid to that plan by destroying everything the Castillero family held dear. "You have heard of the Spanish Armada?" she asked, amused by the predictable puzzled frowns on both foreign faces.

"Of course," the Englishman replied. "Hundreds of years ago, in Elizabethan times, Spain tried to invade England. The plan was a huge failure."

"*Bueno*. You must understand," she replied. "Spaniards hold a different view. It's true the fleet was lost but, for us, the Armada was a glorious endeavor. More than one of our family's ancestors sailed on those ships and never returned. The tales of their courage and sacrifice have been handed down for generations."

She was pleased that both strangers seemed fascinated by her story, so she paused to keep them in suspense.

"That still doesna explain..." the Scot began.

Intending to exhort patience, she made the mistake of touching a fingertip to his lips. She wasn't sure exactly what passed between them, but something smoldering in his eyes told her life would never be the same. Was her earlier premonition coming true?

∽

Payton struggled to resist the temptation to suck Juana's finger into his mouth. "I'm impatient," he confessed, doubting she fully understood his urgent need to suckle the little nipples poking at her shirt. Telling the tale of her family's history had relaxed and excited her. "Go on," he rasped, heeding Kenneth's glare. "Sorry I interrupted."

"The sailors who returned to Spain aboard the few ships that came home told of ferocious storms that drove many vessels onto the treacherous rocks of the Scottish coastline. Over the centuries, the families of the men lost in those shipwrecks nurtured the myth that some may have survived. It's highly unlikely. If they didn't drown, they were probably hanged by the locals. However, the notion of a pilgrimage to Scotland eventually came to fruition in the late seventeen hundreds. My father and his brothers went to Mull because of the legend of a Spanish ship finding shelter there. They knew our ancestors sailed on a vessel with the same name—*San Juan de Sicilia*."

"If your father married one of the locals, I take it they were given a warm welcome," Kenneth quipped.

"Och, aye," Juana replied, glancing quickly at her father when she realized what she'd said.

"I fell in love with Olivia the moment I set eyes on her," Juan said sadly. "She didn't serve the fate I brought her to here."

"Her death wasn't your fault, Papa," Juana said. "The enemy is solely to blame for that atrocity."

Her father seemed lost in thought for a few minutes before he spoke again. "Olivia always missed her homeland. It's the reason she named our daughter..." He narrowed his eyes. "*No importa*. Never mind."

"She named you after her country?" Payton asked.

"My first name is María."

Payton's disappointment must have been written on his face.

"Every girl born in Spain is called María," she explained with a smile. "The name I am known by is Alba."

"Alba," he rasped, savoring the ancient, hallowed name on his lips. "I'm Payton King."

MEANWHILE, BACK IN SCOTLAND

Maureen Hawkins-Graham was too agitated to sleep. "I'm overjoyed Daisy decided to come to Scotland," she told her husband. "But the news about Kenneth is devastating."

Her frantic heart calmed a little when Jock cuddled into her back and cupped her breast.

"I dinna understand why he would go to Spain," he said.

"Daisy said he's been moody and restless since his return from Scotland. I'm convinced he's pining for Cat. Perhaps he saw Spain as a chance to escape his torment."

"And here she is in Scotland, longing for him. Seems silly they canna wed."

"I see no reason they can't," she replied. "We just have to convince them of that."

"Aye. Poor lass hasna stopped cryin' since she found out he's gone to Spain."

"We must do something to bring them together."

"Weel, ye canna take Cat to Spain."

"No, but I could take her to London so she'll be there when he returns."

"Daisy willna be too happy to go back to London so soon."

"I must admit I'm astonished my daughter came, and she does seem content to be here. She's accompanied me to the distillery every day since her arrival."

"Gregor thinks she's sweet on Niven," he said.

"My brother still assumes he knows everything," she snorted in reply. "The older he gets, the dafter his opinions."

～

"I still dinna understand how you could allow Payton to go off to Spain," Tavish shouted from the far end of the distillery's malting floor.

Niven bristled. Hand-turning malt wasn't his favorite pastime and his older brother's accusation stung. "Since when has Payton ever listened to me?" he retorted. "He didna e'en discuss it wi' me."

"Foolhardy, the pair o' them. I thought Kenneth had more sense," Tavish muttered.

Niven gritted his teeth. "First of all, ye must realize Payton has gone to Spain for ye. He doesna really care about sherry barrels, but he kens ye have yer heart set on the plan."

Tavish paused, seemingly considering what Niven had suggested. "And what about our cousin? I ken he's an investor in the distillery, but still."

"I think Kenneth decided to go because he's unhappy. He misses Cat Neish."

"So, ye think 'tis true that Kenneth and Cat care for one another?"

"I do."

"Aunty Maureen has been plotting how to get them together. Too late now."

"Dinna say that," Niven replied, swallowing the lump of dread in his throat. "We hafta assume they'll come back safely."

"Aye. On another topic, how did ye persuade Daisy to come north?"

"I didna. She suggested it."

"She's always been adamant she wouldna come. I wonder what changed her mind?"

Niven didn't care for the way his brother wiggled his eyebrows. "Who can understand why lasses act the way they do?"

"Are ye that obtuse, laddie? 'Tis ye she's pursuing."

"Are ye daft?" he replied. "She's our cousin."

"Lots o' folk marry cousins," Tavish asserted. "'Tis expected in some circles."

∼

When Tavish returned home that evening, he welcomed his wife's kisses. He thanked God once more for a wife who was always glad to see him. It was a far cry from his youth when his parents had forever been at each other's throats.

He took his infant son from his wife's arms and rocked him. "Niven said something that bothered me today," he told Piper, blessed to have a wife he could confide in. "He claims Payton has gone to Spain for my sake."

"Well," she replied, poking at the logs burning in the wood-stove. "Payton knows how important those sherry barrels are to you."

"But to risk his life in order to retrieve them?"

"You should be humbled that he and Kenneth both think your plan to age whisky in sherry barrels is important enough to take the risk."

The knot in his gut tightened. "Let's hope I'm right, then," he replied, tickling Munro under the chin.

"What else did Niven have to say? Anything about Daisy?"

He lifted his laughing son high in the air. "He doesna believe she is interested in him."

His wife chuckled. "He's either lying or blind."

∼

DAISY WAS SURPRISED to find the workings of the distillery very interesting. She actually enjoyed accompanying her mother. At first, the aroma of the malting barley was overwhelming but she soon began to look forward to inhaling it. While her primary motive was to see Niven, she was also glad of the opportunity to get to know Cat Neish.

Tavish King constantly praised the efficient way Cat kept the ledgers up to date and obviously valued her as an employee. Daisy felt ashamed of her long-held assumption that Highland women were uneducated. She began to understand what Kenneth saw in Cat. She was beautiful, intelligent and friendly. But did she love Daisy's brother enough to embark on the challenging life of being a duchess?

There was only one way to find out. "Do you love Kenneth?" she asked Cat one morning when they were alone together in the distillery's makeshift office.

"And I thought Scots were direct," Cat replied with a smile.

"I'm serious," Daisy insisted. "He works hard to continue the success of his dukedom. At least, he used to until…well…until he met you."

"My life hasna been the same since, either," Cat said with a sigh. "I canna seem to stop thinking about him. I'm so afraid something terrible will happen to him in Spain."

"I share your fear," Daisy confessed. "And I think you should go to him when he returns. See what becomes of your relationship."

"Ye think 'tis just a passing fancy?"

"You'll never know unless you go to London. He can't leave England to live here, so…"

They startled when Daisy's mother suddenly appeared and declared, "I think that's a very good idea. I'll speak to Tavish about finding a replacement for you so Daisy and I can take you to England."

"You go, Mama," Daisy replied, surprising herself with what she was about to say. "I'd prefer to stay here a while longer."

Attraction

Four days after their arrival in Gibraltar, Payton and Kenneth found themselves in a hilltop forest on the outskirts of the town of Jerez. Juan warned that other Spanish patriots would probably join them. "The French often march to the east and south of our town," the Spaniard explained. "They bring reinforcements from Sevilla to the troops besieging Cádiz."

"So, this is a good place to lay an ambush," Kenneth replied.

"*Sí*," Alba confirmed with a smile. "We have a better use for the weapons."

"Yonder our *bodega*," Juan said, pointing westward to a ruin, beyond which lay acres of charred vines. "When we get closer, you will see new growth on the vines. It takes more than a few French firebrands to thwart Mother Nature."

"*Verdad*," a stranger said as he sauntered into the camp. "It's *true*."

Payton and his cousin whirled to face the frowning

man they hadn't heard approach, but Juan didn't turn around.

"General Ballesteros," Alba explained softly. "He is more or less the leader of all our little bands."

To the general, she said, "These friends are Payton King and Kenneth Hawkins."

Ballesteros glared at her, probably upset she had revealed their names, but then he shifted his gaze to Kenneth. "Kenny Hawkins? What on earth are you doing here? I haven't seen you since Oxford."

"Manuel?" Kenneth replied. "Good Lord!"

∽

ALBA WAS as surprised as anyone that the *Generalissimo* and Kenneth knew each other from their university days. At first, she was amused by their tales of shared experiences and opinions of various professors. However, as the evening wore on and more of Ballesteros' men drifted into the camp, she began to feel conspicuous as the only person not drinking *vino*. She noticed Payton was strangely silent. He was normally a good conversationalist but seemed to have nothing to contribute to a discussion of university shenanigans.

When she got up and walked away from the gathering, he followed a minute or two later.

"You're quiet this evening," she told him as he sat beside her on a fallen log.

"I need a wee dram o' whisky to loosen my tongue," he quipped.

"Aye, the local *vino* isn't to everyone's taste. It's a

coincidence that your companion knows Ballesteros," she whispered.

"Aye. The world is smaller than we think. He was at school with John Smith as well. I suppose the sons of many wealthy families went to these famous schools."

It was clear from the hint of melancholy in his voice he was not one of those privileged sons.

They sat in silence for long minutes. It was comfortable, yet there was an unspoken tension between them.

"Ye must find it difficult to come back here," he finally said.

"I do," she confessed. "Although there is a delicious irony in using our ruined *bodega* as a base to attack the enemy."

"So, ye're able to get inside?"

"We'll go later, after the General's men complete their next ambush. A French column is on its way from Sevilla. There'll be weapons to add to our collection. Some of our guerrillas are probably in the *bodega* now rearming themselves under cover of darkness."

"Ye stash the weapons ye capture in the ruins?"

"Aye. Muskets, pistols and swords are hidden deep in the cellar where the French never ventured."

"Ye amaze me, Alba," he declared with a smile that melted her insides.

She was drawn to this burly Scot and she sensed he liked her but, sadly, thanks to Napoleon, there was no future for them.

Payton was confused. It wasn't unusual for his manhood to respond wholeheartedly to a lass. However, the lasses he was drawn to were normally well-endowed in the breast department. Alba was painfully thin. He supposed part of the reason lay in living life on the run. Aside from that, he suspected she would never be big up top even if she lived a lavish lifestyle. His cock obviously didn't care. She might be thin, but her body was lithe and fit.

He was ashamed of wanting her so badly. There was Jasmine to consider. God willing, he and Kenneth would return to England. There was no future for Payton King and a Spanish warrior he craved.

He tried to analyze what it was about her that had ensnared him. She was courageous and intelligent, no doubt as a result of her Scottish blood! He admired her. How his brothers would laugh! Payton King admiring a lass!

"Something amusing?" she asked.

"Nay, not really," he replied, realizing he'd chuckled aloud. "I was just thinkin' I'm a lucky man, sittin' here on a warm night beside a beautiful Spanish lass."

"No one has ever told me I am beautiful," she whispered, turning her enormous dark eyes on him.

It struck him then how cruel fate had been to deprive her of a normal life. No suitors, no handsome young Spaniards competing for her hand. He wished he could right that wrong, but he couldn't. "I'd gladly ask yer father's permission to woo ye," he said.

He knew he'd misspoken yet again when she smiled and tears welled in her eyes. "I would like that," she whispered.

He clenched his fists. "But I'm promised to an English lass back home. Jasmine's her name."

"I understand," she replied as she gathered her shawl around her shoulders and scrambled to stand. "It would never work between us anyway."

~

It was foolish to feel jealous of an Englishwoman Alba had never met. Foolish to want Payton for herself. In a few hours, she'd be participating in the latest ambush. She could be killed or, worse still, captured by the French. She had nothing to offer the Scot, not even a voluptuous set of breasts like most girls her age boasted of.

Still, she'd thought he was attracted to her. Men had lusted for her before. She knew the signs. Payton's musky scent gave away his desire, but what she'd seen in his gaze wasn't lust. It was wanting, craving.

But he was promised to a woman named Jasmine. She should have known such a beautiful man would be spoken for.

Choking back tears, she edged closer to the men gathered around the fire.

"*¿Qué pasa, hija?*" her father asked.

"Nothing's wrong, Papa," she lied, expecting him to censure her for sitting alone with Payton.

"You like the Scot," he replied. "And he likes you."

Too heartsick to keep up the pretense, she nodded. "You're right, but he's betrothed."

As usual, his face betrayed no emotion. It was impossible to discern his reaction. After a few minutes, he spoke again. "Nevertheless, I'm going to ask him to take you to Scotland."

Winged creatures took flight in her belly. "But..."

"You will be safer with your mother's sister in Mull until the war is over."

"But I want to fight with you, Papa. I want to avenge Mama."

"You've already done more than enough to satisfy that," he replied. "Your Mama would want you to live and be happy. And I'll feel better knowing you are safe."

Traveling to Scotland with a man she wanted but couldn't have would be torture, but at least she'd be away from the carnage. She'd always wanted to visit her mother's homeland. "He might not agree," she said.

"He will."

Ambush

"I feel superfluous," Kenneth said.

"I ken what ye mean," Payton replied. "They've given us pistols and muskets, but I doubt our contribution will add much firepower to the hundred or so guerrillas they've mustered."

"Here we are," Kenneth added. "Armed to the teeth, lying on our bellies in wait for a French column to pass through the gully below our vantage point. It's strange, but I've never felt more alive."

A commotion behind them caught their attention. Twenty men were heaving on ropes. Eventually, thanks to their efforts, a gun carriage lurched its way out of the bushes, Ballesteros striding along beside it, one hand on the cannon.

"Where did you get that?" Kenneth exclaimed to his university chum.

"Captured from the French. Napoleon has the best artillery—lightweight, easy to move, if you have horses!"

Kenneth wondered how the Spaniards moved the piece from place to place. "I've heard as much about the French artillery," he replied. "They say it's the principal reason for the Emperor's military success."

Ballesteros agreed. "However, in Spain his army can only use the eight pounder, like this one. The terrain here is too rugged for the rest of the famous Gribeauval artillery. They do have the larger siege cannons pointed at Cádiz. When they are forced to abandon the siege, they'll have a devil of a time taking those cannon with them."

"Ye think the siege will fail?" Payton asked.

"They haven't managed to capture the port in almost two years, even though they have it more or less surrounded. Of course, we've had a hand in their difficulties."

~

BALLESTEROS' quip was an understatement. A foreign army far from home couldn't hope to win against an enemy that knew the difficult terrain and was willing to lug heavy cannon to wherever it was needed. The determination to be victorious was writ plain on every swarthy face. Payton had learned from conversations with Alba and her father that Spaniards were proud of their country, their religion and their monarchy. They weren't about to let the Corsican upstart rule them by proxy through his brother installed as the puppet king in Madrid. Kenneth told him Ballesteros was the son of a

Spanish duke, which explained his attendance at an English university. In this war, noblemen and common folk alike were united in the cause of ousting the invader.

Payton understood what Kenneth meant about feeling alive. Preparing to aid in the ambush of armed French soldiers, his gut was in knots. At least he was fighting for something worthwhile. Everyone around him must be equally terrified, but you wouldn't know it. Even Alba, lying in the grass not ten feet away from him, her musket sighted on the valley below, seemed composed. He hadn't noticed her endearing little bottom before.

When she turned her head to smile at him, he fought the overwhelming urge to scoop her up and carry her away—far away to a place of safety.

~

Mixed emotions swirled through Alba. Fear tightened her innards. She should be used to the violence by now, but did anyone really ever get used to it?

The turmoil in her heart was worse. She'd become resigned to the life of a partisan. She was a comrade, a freedom fighter. A secure home, a family and a man who loved her—these were things the French invasion had taken away and she'd accepted that reality.

Payton King had reawakened buried dreams and desires. She should resent him for it, but couldn't. Seeking safety in Scotland was appealing, though perhaps it would be easier on her heart to stay in Spain and go on fighting—until she lost her life or until the French were sent packing.

She glanced across at the Scot while the men were preparing the cannon. He tried to mask his fear with a smile, but she would be surprised and even disappointed if he wasn't afraid.

She had a fanciful notion to beg him to carry her off to a place of safety. But her future was here and now in this valley whose peaceful beauty was about to be soaked in blood. Safety in the strong arms of Payton King wasn't an option.

～

Payton experienced a momentary twinge of pity for the immaculately uniformed French soldiers marching behind their mounted officers. Their bayonets were fixed, but that would do them no good against the cannon that was primed to send them to hell.

"They're nervous," Kenneth whispered.

"Ye'd be scannin' the hillsides too," Payton replied. "The Spaniards havena attacked in this valley before, but the French must realize it could happen anywhere in these hills."

"Manuel told me they aim to mow down the infantry without killing the packhorses carrying weapons."

Payton's generation hadn't fought in clan wars, but he now appreciated how his ancestors must have felt lying in wait for an enemy clan. "The Kings are a sept o' Clan MacGregor," he reminded his cousin. "They knew what this kind of warfare was all about."

"More than most other clans, I understand," Kenneth replied.

Payton found it interesting that his cousin had evidently been doing some research. "Aye. They were persecuted, so they nay doot knew how the French feel right now."

He'd steeled himself for the cannon's boom, but reminiscing about Clan MacGregor had distracted him. For one terrible moment, he thought the ordnance had exploded like King James' *Mons Meg* at the siege of Roxburgh. Gooseflesh marched up his spine when the grapeshot found its mark and the screaming began in the valley below. Jaw clenched, he scrambled to his feet and rushed downhill to help the guerrillas finish off anyone not blown to bits.

He'd been nervous about killing men, something he'd never had to do before. Was it the Viking blood in his veins that surged when he joined the mayhem? There was something horribly satisfying about plunging a bayonet into the belly of a man intent on killing you. He wasn't Spanish, didn't even speak the language, but he yelled *España* as loudly as anyone until he was hoarse.

He gulped air, ready to fall to his knees when the smoke cleared and silence suddenly reigned. Relieved to see Kenneth still on his feet, he slung the musket over his shoulder, patted the pistol in his waistband that he hadn't made use of, and cast about for Alba.

The MacGregor war-cry came to his lips when he saw a sniggering French officer with his sword raised. He had disarmed Alba and was intending to run her through.

Àrd-Choille, he yelled as he rushed forward and fired his pistol.

Chin quivering, eyes filled with terror, Alba stared at the dead soldier.

When she swooned, Payton prevented her fall and carried her back up the hill.

THE BODEGA

In the aftermath of the conflict, Kenneth helped bury the Spanish dead, did what he could for the wounded, and drank too much of the French brandy discovered among the pillaged goods. He had never seen an automaton, but knew of an elaborate picture with mechanical figures created for Madame de la Pompadour. He swallowed his horror when the guerrillas bayoneted the surviving French officers. It made sense to his dulled brain that they didn't want to waste musket balls. It was probably also true that the French would have taken no prisoners had they been victorious.

Payton seemed to be in the same kind of stupor, though he'd declined the brandy and never left Alba's side.

Despite the fog in Kenneth's brain, one thing had become crystal clear. He loved Catriona Neish and was determined to make her his, society's rules be damned.

The decision brought a peaceful calm he hadn't felt since—well, never.

Anxious to share his epiphany with Payton, he hesitated when his cousin left Alba's side and came toward him, his brow furrowed. The Spanish woman was awake and talking, so Kenneth assumed she was going to recover. "What's amiss?" he asked.

"I need yer advice," Payton replied.

"A Scot asking a Sassenach for advice?" Kenneth quipped, aware the self-assured Payton would never have asked had it not been important.

"Alba's father wants us to take her with us when we leave Spain. He thinks she'll be safer with her aunty in Mull."

Kenneth saw the merit in the plan, yet Payton seemed troubled by it. His growing conviction that his cousin cared deeply about Alba was obviously correct. "The prospect of taking her with us worries you."

Payton met his gaze. "I am falling in love with her, but I'm promised."

Kenneth hadn't known Payton long and they'd never been close friends. But he understood the heartbreak of a man wanting a woman he thought he couldn't have. If Payton and Alba were meant to be—and any fool could see the petite warrior and the giant Scot were good together—the Duke of Ramsay was going to do everything in his power to help them. "We'll see her safely to Scotland," he promised.

PAYTON AND THE PASSIONATE PARTISAN

Despite his own inner turmoil, Payton sensed a change in his cousin's demeanor. "Ye've made a decision about Cat."

"Is it that obvious?" Kenneth chuckled. "I'm going to ask her to marry me."

Payton shook his cousin's hand. "Good. She'll be a grand duchess."

"I do believe you're right," Kenneth replied. "Are you sure about Jasmine?"

Payton bristled. "I promised to wed her and I'm a man o' my word."

"But Alba's the one you want."

"A man canna always have what he wants."

"I believed that for a long time. I'm older and wiser now!"

Payton appreciated the jest, but his gut was in knots. "It makes sense to take Alba away from this war."

"Then we'll do it," Kenneth retorted. "Surely her safety is what's important."

"Aye," he agreed, though it would be easier on his heart to leave her behind.

He acknowledged inwardly that wasn't true. If he left her in Spain, he'd spend his life worrying about what might have happened to her. Jaw clenched, he turned away to speak to Alba's father.

~

Her heart in knots, Alba trudged along with her comrades. Returning to her family's ruined *bodega* was gut-wrenching, but she understood the necessity. The cellar beneath the *bodega* hid all manner of useful provisions and provided a place of refuge for the weary guerrillas.

This visit might prove to be her undoing. Payton would quickly become aware this was, in fact, the *bodega* that had received the barrel staves. He would wonder why they hadn't told him the truth. Committing to take her to Scotland had already alienated him. He obviously didn't want to agree, but no amount of protest on her part would deter her father—nor Kenneth for that matter. Payton had avoided her throughout the long walk from the site of the ambush to the vineyard.

If she were honest with herself, she longed to escape with Payton, not for safety's sake, but because the prospect of saying goodbye forever was intolerable. He was promised to another, but they could be friends who cared about each other. Couldn't they?

She came to an abrupt halt. Her father, Payton and Kenneth stood together in front of the *bodega*. They were looking up at the scorched sign that had once proudly announced the property belonged to *Bodegas Castillero*. Half of it was missing, but part of the family name was still visible.

Payton turned to her, an unexpected smile on his face. "We suspected as much," he confessed.

"The less you know, the safer for everyone," Alba's father said. "But I can admit now that I'm Pedro Castillero."

Alba breathed more easily when the men shook hands and slapped each other on the back like three long-lost friends.

It gladdened her heart that her Papa liked and trusted Payton to deliver her to Mull. But could she trust herself in his presence?

~

Most of the interior of the *bodega* was in ruins. Shards of glass and wood from shattered barrels covered the stone floor.

"It's not usually red," Pedro explained sadly. "Most of the stain is from the sherry they didn't drink."

"I'd love to have seen this place in operation," Payton declared. "So would my older brother, Tavish. He's the master distiller."

"One day, perhaps, we will rebuild and life will go back to normal."

Payton fully understood the wistful hopelessness in Pedro's voice. In the midst of so much wanton destruction, normalcy seemed unattainable. "It's been a while since ye made sherry here, but I can still detect the aroma o' spirits."

"That's the *flor* you smell," Alba explained.

"I've heard of that," Kenneth interjected. "It's a yeasty growth unique to this area of Spain."

"Yes, the climate encourages its growth on top of the fermenting grapes," Pedro said. "We call it the *misterio de la bodega*. It's what makes our *fino* sherry special."

"So, did you use the barrels we sent?" Payton asked.

"*Sí*, indeed," Pedro replied. "We were so impressed with the way your staves were made, we started to copy them when we needed to replace barrels."

"I dinna suppose any survived the French?"

"*Bueno*," Pedro replied. "The enemy sees only what is right under his long nose."

"We had a second hidden *solera*," Alba explained.

"*Solera*?" Kenneth asked.

"An array of barrels arranged in a hierarchy, with the younger wines partially replacing the older wines as they are taken out."

"Our barrels are still in this *solera*?"

"*Sí*."

GOODBYE CAT

Standing with Jock, Daisy and Gregor outside the house in Glengeárr where she'd grown up, Maureen noted the progress made by the workmen repointing the stone walls. Since moving back into Lockie House a few months ago, she and Jock had undertaken a great many repairs. With most of the rooms renovated and refurbished, the old house was now very comfortable. Reluctant to leave all the comforts of her former life behind, she'd hired trustworthy servants. She was loath to leave, even for this important journey to London.

The capital city held bittersweet memories of a life lived as the dignified duchess of a man she loved, a man who'd unexpectedly inherited a dukedom. She'd risen to the challenges, but realized now it had been at the cost of her Scottishness. But Freddie was gone now and she was happy with a new husband and a new life back where she'd been born.

However, her present duty was to do what she could to ensure the happiness of her son.

Seeking a distraction, she turned her attention to the shiny carriage parked in front of the house. "I never liked Dalwhinnie when he was a viscount," she declared. "He's even more pompous now he's succeeded his father as Earl of Craigdarroch. But it was good of him to lend us his vehicle."

"Aye. 'Twill get us to Edinburgh in comfort, then on to the Royal Mail," Jock replied. "The earl takes his investment in the distillery seriously."

"And why not?" Gregor replied in his typical sarcastic fashion. "He's gettin' the tax revenue from the license he granted. Now, mind what I told ye about the mail coach. Ye must insist on seats inside."

Her brother had reminded her at least twenty times, so Maureen wasn't likely to forget. "Don't worry. I've no intention of riding outside on the roof."

"And ye must stay at the White Horse in Edinburgh."

"Already arranged," Jock replied.

"So," Daisy piped up. "We're just waiting for Cat, then you can be off."

"Are you sure you don't want to come with us?" Maureen asked the daughter who'd always resisted the idea of visiting Scotland.

"Positive," Daisy replied. "I'll be fine here."

Maureen and Jock exchanged a glance. Daisy wanted to stay so she could continue her pursuit of Niven King. It was worrisome. Niven hadn't shown much interest in return and Daisy tended to think herself in love for a while before moving on to some other beau. It was exactly what she'd done with Niven's brother, Payton.

Maureen felt she should say something about her daughter's behavior before they departed, but Jock had advised against it. She realized she'd dithered too long when Cat emerged from her cottage down the street, arm in arm with Piper. Tavish carried her valise. Niven tagged along behind.

Maureen wasn't surprised to see Cat had been weeping after saying goodbye to her grandfather. Auld Jamie was failing and it was unlikely his granddaughter would see him again in this life.

∽

CAT WAS TORN. Her grandfather had insisted she accompany Lady Maureen to London, but it was probable she would never see him again. He'd been her only family since the death of her parents ten years before. "Go and be happy," he'd said.

Therein lay her doubts. She loved Kenneth Hawkins, and everyone was convinced he loved her. But could they be happy together? She was an ordinary Highland lass. He was a sophisticated nobleman who carried the weighty responsibility of a dukedom on his shoulders. They'd spent so little time together. Yet the magic between them was powerful.

She'd never been to London, nor even to Edinburgh. The prospect of living in a big city was terrifying.

It might be true that Kenneth loved her, but could he marry a commoner? Perhaps he thought of her more as his *leman*? The notion of becoming his mistress made her blood run cold. She had too much pride to agree to such an arrangement.

"Stop worrying," Piper told her. "If things don't work out, at least you'll have tried. You'd regret it all your life if you don't give Kenneth a chance."

"But what if he doesna return from Spain?"

"We must pray he does," her friend replied. "If he doesn't, you and his mother will be a source of comfort for each other."

"Aye," Tavish agreed as he passed her valise to the driver. "I kent as soon as I set eyes on Piper that she was the lass for me. I suspect 'twas the same for ye and Kenneth. Ye hafta go and find out if there's a future wi' my cousin."

"I dinna ken if I'm brave enough," Cat replied.

"Aye, ye are," Tavish replied.

~

CRAIGDARROCH'S shiny black carriage carrying Lady Maureen, Jock and Cat eventually disappeared from view. Niven risked a glance at Daisy Hawkins. He should have known she'd be staring coyly at him. The knot in his gut tightened. She'd insisted on staying in a place where she really didn't belong so she could continue pursuing him.

Oddly, he was beginning to enjoy her shameless flirtation. Tavish had noticed and sensibly warned him against becoming involved with her. "She'll dump ye like she dumped Payton," his brother cautioned.

On top of that likelihood, Niven could never consider leaving the Highlands permanently. Daisy was doing a grand job of being enthusiastic about the distillery and all things Scottish. But Niven simply couldn't convince himself she possessed the ability to adapt to life in Scotland that Tavish's wife had demonstrated since coming to live in Glengeárr.

While it was true that her mother's Scottish blood ran in Daisy's veins, she comported herself like a haughty English noblewoman. The locals were polite and respectful toward her, but weren't what he'd call friendly.

Still, Tavish had his Piper and their little Munro. Payton was gone, perhaps never to return. If the lass wanted to throw herself at the last unmarried King, who was he to say nay?

FOG

Growing up in the Highlands, Cat was no stranger to mists. They rolled off the mountain tops, adding a touch of mystery and grandeur to the glens and valleys below.

A thick fog greeted the arrival of the mail coach in London. There was nothing mysterious or wonderful about it. It smothered everything like a shroud.

"This is Piccadilly," Lady Maureen explained as they disembarked. "Not that we can see anything of the busy thoroughfare."

They'd spent so many hours cooped up in the overnight coach, Cat feared her limbs might not work when her feet touched the ground.

The air smelled damp and fetid. The fog crept into her throat. Muffled footsteps and street-sellers' cries indicated there must be people about, but they were all invisible. Hooves clip-clopped, but riders and horses were perhaps a figment of Cat's imagination.

She prayed she'd somehow dreamt all this. When she

opened her eyes, she'd be back in Glengeárr, making supper for her grandfather.

"Dinna be discouraged," Mr. Graham advised, taking her elbow. "London takes some getting used to after the fresh air o' the Highlands."

"Is it always like this?" she asked.

"Heavens, no," Lady Maureen replied. "I'll wager there'll be no fog at all once we leave the city behind."

Cat hoped that were true. She didn't think she could live in a permanent fog.

Within minutes, they had boarded what Mr. Graham referred to as a *hackney*. Cat thanked God for her traveling companions. She could never have made this long, exhausting journey alone. Lady Maureen had taken the opportunity of tedious hours on the road to describe Ramsay House where Kenneth dwelt. To a lass who'd lived all her life in a one-room cottage, it sounded daunting. "But we'll stay at the Dower House, my former home," Lady Maureen explained. "It wouldn't be proper for you to stay in Kenneth's residence just yet."

Lady Maureen had been the Duchess of Ramsay for years until the death of her first husband. She'd warned Cat that Kenneth's role as the duke involved a lot of rules that people expected noble men and women to follow.

"I dinna ken if I'm up to that," she replied.

"I'm confident you'll make a splendid duchess. And I'll help you as much as I can. Remember, I was an ordinary lass from Glengeárr. You've the same Highland backbone that stood me in good stead."

"And ye've got a powerful weapon in yer arsenal," Mr. Graham said. "Ye and Kenneth love each other."

Cat sincerely hoped that were true.

～

THE FOG HAD LIFTED EVEN before they reached the avenue that led to Ramsay House, much to Maureen's relief. Cat's furrowed brow was a clear sign she already regretted the decision to come to London. The mansion itself looked splendid as they drove by on their way to the Dower House. Sun blazed in every window and warmed the limestone.

"It's enormous," Cat sighed. "And only Kenneth lives here?"

"At the moment, yes," Maureen confirmed. "But you and he can fill it with lots of children, and the staff is wonderful."

"Servants, ye mean?"

"You'll get used to having servants, especially once the little ones start arriving."

"'Tis hard to take it all in, and 'twill be for naught if Kenneth doesna return."

Maureen didn't want to consider that dire possibility. "I wish we had some way of letting him know you're in London. He'd be back here in a flash if he knew."

A servant Maureen didn't recognize emerged from the Dower House when they arrived. She supposed he was the new butler appointed in her absence by her son. Her former butler decided to retire when she went to Scotland. "Pontefract, is it?" she asked, nodding to the two familiar footmen who'd accompanied him.

"At your service, Your Grace," he replied with a courteous bow.

"Beggin' yer pardon," Cat whispered. "I havena been usin' yer title."

"And thank goodness for that. I suppose I'll have to get used to it again."

Jock chuckled. "Just so long as ye dinna expect me to address ye thus."

"I expect you're worn out after your journey," the butler said as they entered the foyer. "Mrs. Pontefract has the rooms aired out and ready."

Tired as she was, Maureen had forgotten the butler came with a wife who'd taken over as Head Housekeeper. "That sounds splendid," she replied as a diminutive woman came forward. "Take Miss Neish to her room first, Mrs. Pontefract. I know the way to my chambers."

"Sleep," she commanded Cat. "On the morrow, we'll go to Bond Street to shop for new outfits for you."

Cat shook her head. "I canna..."

"Yes, you can and you must let me do this for you... and for Kenneth."

～

"If Lady Daisy Hawkins could see me now," Jasmine thought as she strolled along Bond Street on Lord Justin Carmichael's arm. The only fly in the ointment was her lady's maid who tagged along behind. Jasmine's mother had insisted they must take Clara as a chaperone.

It was the third time Justin had taken her shopping. He was ever so generous and didn't seem to mind spending his money on whatever she took a fancy to buying. Of course, he'd inherited a wealthy earldom and kept dropping hints about looking for a wife now he had an obligation to sire an heir.

By rights, she should tell him about her betrothal to Payton King, but her mother had forbidden it. Payton might never come back from Spain in any case, and Justin was rich. Not only that, he took liberties when the sullen Clara wasn't paying attention, which was most of the time. Payton had never touched her breasts and she liked feeling tingly all over when Justin brushed his thumb over a nipple.

"It's Miss Foxworthy, isn't it?"

Jolted from her wanton thoughts, she turned to see Daisy Hawkins' mother in the company of a dark-haired woman who put Jasmine in mind of a gypsy. "Yes, Your Grace," she replied, suddenly aware of Justin's curiosity. "May I introduce the Earl of Waterdown?"

"Duchess," Justin said, bestowing a courtly kiss.

"Waterdown," the older woman replied, one eyebrow raised, obviously aware his failure to address her as *Your Grace* had established him as a member of the nobility. "Let me make known to you both Miss Catriona Neish. She's from Glengeárr and knows Miss Foxworthy's fiancé very well."

"I'm pleased to meet ye," Miss Neish said. "We're all prayin' for Payton's safe return from Spain."

Heat flooded Jasmine from head to toe. She wanted to wipe the smirk off Clara's face. Rooted to the spot, and not knowing what to say, she was grateful when Justin tapped his beaver and bade the others good-day.

"Don't worry," he said softly as he escorted her down Bond Street. "I'm sure I can compete with this absentee Scotsman."

"You already knew about him, didn't you?"

"I know everything about you, Jasmine."

The notion was at once thrilling and a not a little scary.

HARD WORK

Pedro and Alba led the way through the *caverna* beneath the *bodega*. Payton had never seen a cellar like it. The ceiling where he and his brothers stored the *Uachdaran* whisky barrels was so low, he had to stoop to avoid banging his head. Here, arched columns soared high overhead. It was more like a cathedral than a cellar.

But the rampage of wanton destruction had continued even in this hallowed place. He closed his eyes and imagined the bustling activity that must have gone on here before the invasion.

Alba pointed to an array of a dozen damaged barrels stacked in three layers on a metal frame. "This is a *solera* but, as you see, the French hacked open the barrels and spilled the sherry."

Payton opened his eyes. "But these old barrels aren't the ones we sent," he said, hoping he didn't sound too disappointed.

Pedro squeezed his body between the back of the

ruined *solera* and the wall. "Follow me and Alba," he replied with a smile.

Payton feared he and Kenneth might end up wedged for all eternity in the narrow space as they inched their way behind the barrels. Alba had no trouble leading the way to an ancient wooden doorway. "Our enemies never discovered this," Pedro boasted, as he twisted his body and put his shoulder to the door.

"I'm not surprised," Kenneth replied. "It's well hidden."

They soon found themselves in another cellar, smaller, but with a similar vaulted ceiling. In one corner, set out in meticulous order, was a cache of weapons—sabres, muskets, pistols and a few English rifles.

"Well, douse my toplights," Kenneth exclaimed. "You weren't joking."

Looking slightly puzzled, but still smiling proudly, Pedro nodded to the far wall.

"Our barrels," Payton declared, his heart beating wildly. "A hidden *solera*."

"*Sí*," Pedro confirmed. "The problem is, they are full of the only sherry we have left."

∾

BARED TO THE WAIST, Kenneth wiped the sweat from his brow with his kerchief. "I have to admit, Cousin," he told Payton. "I've never worked so hard in my life."

As soon as the words were spoken, he realized he was talking to a well-muscled man who'd spent years turning malting barley by hand. Payton had trudged through

Highland bogs digging peat and had probably lugged around more barrels than Kenneth had ever seen.

"Don't misunderstand," he added. "It feels good to have spent a week doing something productive. I've learned how to make new barrels out of broken pieces of old ones, how to rebuild a *solera* and transfer sherry from one barrel to another."

"All useful skills for a duke," Payton replied with a wink.

"Haw, haw," Kenneth replied, knowing his cousin meant no offense. "Seriously, when I get back to England, I'm not going to sit around on my arse every day. It's time I got hands-on with various projects I've let Mainwaring supervise."

"I ken how ye feel," Payton agreed. "I've learned a lot about making sherry which could prove useful in the future. I just wish 'twasna so infernally hot. I'm nay used to the heat."

"I suppose August is high summer here. Certainly hotter than England."

They left their tasks and hurried inside upon hearing a whistled signal from a nearby look-out.

Pedro joined them a few minutes later. "Curious," he said. "They've spotted the third French column heading for Sevilla in as many days. It's odd that they are hauling cannon. I wouldn't be surprised if Ballesteros has his eye on them."

Payton followed the others outside when the all-clear came. He'd been working bare-chested all afternoon but he and Kenneth hastily donned their shirts when Alba came into the courtyard.

"I thought you might like to see something of the house," she said. "Most of the furniture is ruined, but…"

"You go with her, Payton," Kenneth said. "I'm going to sit in the shade for a while."

It seemed his cousin was intent on encouraging a relationship between him and Alba, despite Payton's frequent reminders of his commitment to Jasmine.

"I want to show you the gallery of my ancestors," Alba cajoled.

How could a man resist those soulful eyes? "*Adelante*," he replied, hoping he'd remembered the correct Spanish word.

Her smile relieved his apprehension.

She led him quickly through smoke-blackened rooms where the smell of charred wood lingered. He helped her sidestep splintered beams that had fallen to the floor. They eventually arrived in a long hallway. "There used to be portraits of my ancestors all along this wall," she said. "Now, as you see, there are just these few."

Payton surveyed the wreckage of her family history. The remaining portraits all hung askew, their frames damaged. "I'm so sorry," he said softly, taking hold of her hand.

She studied their joined hands, but didn't pull away. "This is my Spanish grandfather, Antonio Castillero," she said, pointing to the nearest portrait. "Of course, there was never a painting of my Scottish grandfather."

He'd been reluctant to agree to taking her to Scotland, but the idea suddenly made sense. "Ye'll mayhap meet him in the flesh when ye get to Mull."

He knew he'd said the wrong thing when tears welled in her eyes. It was wrong, but how could a man resist? He took her into his arms.

"I'll have to tell Mama's family how she died," she said hoarsely.

Payton could muster no reply, his thoughts wholly on the lithe little body pressed to his. "Forgive me," he whispered. "I've been working in the hot sun all afternoon."

"*Me hueles maravilloso,*" she said, inhaling deeply as she nuzzled her nose into his chest.

He didn't understand the Spanish, but the sultriness in her voice made it clear what she meant. She too smelled wonderful.

Seized by urges he should control, he lifted her. Desire took hold when she twined her legs around his hips and her arms around his neck. He kissed her, savoring her warmth when she allowed his tongue entry into her mouth. He couldn't explain it, but he'd never wanted a woman more than he wanted this courageous Spaniard.

∼

CLINGING TO HER SCOT, Alba suckled his tongue and let him breathe for her. His skin smelled of hard work, and something else—something uniquely masculine.

It was wrong to want him. He belonged to another.

But here, in this beloved gallery where so much had been taken from her, she would accept whatever he could give her. "*Te amo*, Payton," she whispered when they broke apart for breath.

His puzzled frown confirmed that he didn't understand the foreign words.

"I want ye," he growled, cupping his hands under her bottom.

She was an innocent, but had lived among men for so long she recognized the hard flesh pressed against her most intimate place as male arousal. Peasants often boasted of their sexual prowess when they thought she couldn't hear. When Alba turned sixteen, her mother explained what happened between a husband and wife. Then, her parents assumed she would soon marry.

But she and Payton could never marry. "*Lo siento*," she said, pulling away. "I'm sorry."

She fled before he could stop her.

VIVA CADIZ

A thousand conflicting thoughts flew through Payton's mind. He was fond of Jasmine Foxworthy but she'd never set him alight, never made him feel the love he felt now for Alba. Was it love? Or just an overwhelming need to protect and cherish a woman who'd lost so much? She certainly didn't have the tempting figure Jasmine possessed, yet he burned to bury himself inside Alba.

She'd told him in her own language that she loved him, no doubt thinking he wouldn't understand. Her confession had caused an uproar in his loins.

He lingered in the gallery until he had his breathing and his manhood under better control.

An unexpected scene greeted him when he regained the courtyard. For a week, Pedro had made sure not one drop of the precious sherry was spilled during the transfer to the reclaimed barrels. Now, every man had a tumbler in his hand. There was laughter. Men slapped each other on the back. Accompanied by a guitar, two fellows danced a *sevillana* together, one acting the provocative part of the female partner. The raucous audience clapped enthusiastically as castanets clicked.

"*Señor* Payton," Pedro exclaimed when he saw him. "The French, they have abandoned Cádiz."

"Imagine," Kenneth shouted. "The first city to withstand a Napoleonic siege."

"Ballesteros brought the news," Alba explained. "It's the reason the French have been sending troops north. It seems Wellington was victorious at Salamanca. A combined British, Spanish and Portuguese force has entered Madrid and is now marching to Burgos. The enemy risks being surrounded if they remain here in Andalucía."

"So, the war is over?" Payton asked.

"Far from it, unfortunately," Ballesteros replied as he joined the group. "The French still control most of the north, so we will fight on. Now, we go to Cádiz. I'm told the French have left their siege cannons behind."

Payton was elated for the Spanish victory. The war wasn't over, but at least that meant he and Kenneth would still be expected to take Alba with them when they sailed away. He should refuse, but knew he couldn't.

~

THE FRENCH WITHDRAWAL from Cádiz proved to Alba that victory was possible. Her countrymen and women would continue the fight, and she should be part of it. After the destruction of the *bodega* and her mother's murder, she'd willingly embraced the danger of patriotic resistance. With nothing left to live for except a Spain free of the French, she was numb to the threat of death.

Payton King had changed that. He'd awakened feelings and emotions she supposed every young woman experiences in times of peace. She didn't want to abandon those feelings, though she knew they would eventually lead to a broken heart. She wanted to live.

She was intoxicated with him. The irony was inescapable—a whisky distiller and a sherry heiress. But her inheritance had been destroyed, so there was nothing left to lose by going to Scotland. Nothing to gain either, except a few more weeks with a man she craved. She'd be exchanging the torment of war with the agony of heartbreak.

"Alba."

Her father's voice jolted her back to the courtyard. "Papa."

"*Señor* Kenneth has a brilliant idea."

The blushing Englishman stood beside her father. "Not brilliant, but a possibility."

"What is it?" she replied, wondering if sunburn was perhaps the reason for his red face.

"Payton and I have been contemplating the best way of transporting the barrels to Gibraltar," he said. "We'd more or less decided to break them apart and load the staves onto mules."

She too had worried about the difficulties inherent in the mission. "It might not be as dangerous now the French are withdrawing from Andalucía."

"That's just it. If they've abandoned Cádiz, why not

take the barrels there, load them on a ship and sail to Gibraltar?"

"And I've agreed they can take one barrel of our sherry with them to England," her father declared proudly.

∼

Most of the Spaniards left with Ballesteros. Kenneth couldn't blame them. No one wanted to help prepare and load empty barrels for shipment when they could be off to Cádiz. Site of Spain's provisional government after the fall of Madrid, the beleaguered port city would need all the manpower it could get to recover from such a long siege.

Alba and her father stayed behind to assist but Pedro wasn't a young man. He took care of transferring the remaining sherry to his own rebuilt barrels. Alba simply wasn't built for hauling barrels. She took care of snaring rabbits and cooking whatever meager rations she was able to forage.

Payton was as nervous as a rabbit himself whenever Alba was away from the *bodega*.

"Calm down," Kenneth advised his cousin one particularly sultry afternoon when they were both hot and weary. "Alba knows the terrain. She'll be fine."

"I'm just anxious to get these barrels back to Glengeárr."

"You can't fool me," Kenneth replied. "You don't hide your feelings very well."

"Weel. I am relieved we dinna need to break the

barrels down into staves. They could dry out before we got them home, and what use would that be?"

"All right. Have it your way," Kenneth conceded. "In any case, Pedro has left a small amount of sherry in each barrel just to keep the flavor in the wood."

The crack of musket fire brought an abrupt halt to the conversation and sent them diving for cover under the wagon.

"Are you hit?" Kenneth asked, trying valiantly to ignore the blood pouring from his temple.

"Nay. Mayhap they got one of the barrels. But who... ye're bleedin'."

"Just a flesh wound, I think," he replied hopefully. "They say the scalp bleeds profusely."

They stopped talking when three French soldiers crept into the courtyard, but there was nothing for it but to comply when the wagon was surrounded and they were ordered out of hiding.

∼

ALBA HAD ALMOST MADE it back at the *bodega* when she heard the shot. Dropping the rabbits and a pheasant she'd been lucky enough to snare, she crouched on all fours in the long grass and listened. Male voices were speaking French. She'd seen no evidence of the enemy while she'd been out foraging. What were they doing here?

She crept forward and peered into the courtyard. Dizzying fear soared through her body. Hands in the air,

Payton and Kenneth stood with their backs to the wagon. Blood oozed from a wound on Kenneth's head.

Three armed French soldiers were taunting them, clearly believing they were Spaniards. "*Espagnols, cochons,*" they shouted, all the while spitting at the ground.

She prayed the men she cared about kept their mouths shut. The soldiers might toy with Spaniards for a while. They would kill two British men without hesitation.

She couldn't see the faces of the soldiers, but they appeared to be unsteady on their feet.

"*Borrachos,*" she whispered.

Their uniforms were torn and dirty; their boots muddied. Napoleon's army prided itself on the immaculate appearance of its rank and file soldiers.

"Deserters, as well as *drunkards,*" she hissed as she took aim and fired at the loudest of the three.

He crumpled to the ground. The other two turned, wide-eyed and alarmed. Payton and Kenneth rushed forward and overpowered them.

ROYAL NAVY TO THE RESCUE

Two days after the capture of the French deserters, Payton sat on the driver's bench of the wagon, reins in hand. Sporting a bandage around his head, Kenneth sat beside him. Two bad-tempered mules harnessed in the traces brayed their displeasure at the prospect of pulling a heavy load all the way to Cádiz.

Payton couldn't bear to watch the scene unfolding in the doorway of the ruined *bodega*. Pedro and his daughter stood together, locked in a farewell embrace.

When Payton left his own country, he fully intended to return. Alba must know the chances of seeing her beloved father again were remote. He and Kenneth had taken their leave of Pedro before climbing into the wagon. He patted the inner pocket where he'd secreted the small parcel Pedro had given him. He was charged with presenting it to Alba if ever she married.

Ballesteros had sent a contingent of men to help guard the cache of weapons in the *bodega*, so Payton was reassured the Spaniard wouldn't be alone. Nevertheless, it was like saying goodbye to an old friend.

"*Señor* Payton, I am trusting you with the most precious thing in my life," Pedro said. "I know you love her and will keep her safe."

Payton could only nod, unwilling to get into an explanation about Jasmine. He shook Pedro's hand and wished him *Vaya Con Dios*.

It was possible there were other desperate French deserters in the area. Hanging from a makeshift scaffold erected on the hill, the naked bodies of the three who'd attacked the *bodega* would serve as a deterrent.

Payton thought it a macabre memory for Alba to carry with her, but she'd suggested the punishment. He and Kenneth owed their lives to her, so he wasn't about to argue. Perhaps she needed to carry the gruesome sight in her memory. Cruelty and horror had become the hallmark of this war—a circumstance every Scot knew all too well. Cumberland's butchery in the aftermath of Culloden would sit like a stone in the guts of Highlanders for generations to come.

"When are you going to admit you love her?" Kenneth asked unexpectedly.

"If I admit it, then I also have to face the reality I can never have her," he replied.

"You're determined to marry Jasmine?"

Hot and heartsick, Payton had no patience for this conversation. "Ye ken I pledged myself to her."

"And do you suppose Jasmine is living like a nun in your absence?"

Overwhelming sadness crept into Payton's heart but

he couldn't summon an ounce of jealousy when he thought of Jasmine with another man. He was fated to live life with a woman he didn't love and who didn't love him.

He forced a bright, reassuring smile when a tearful Alba broke free of her father and ran to the wagon.

~

Alba felt hollow. Ballesteros had provided an armed escort, but danger still lurked on the road to Cádiz. She was not afraid for herself. Her concern was for the beloved father she might never see again, and for the two brave men who intended to see her safely to Scotland.

She was grateful neither Kenneth nor Payton made any attempt at conversation as they traveled, but Kenneth's gentle arm around her shoulders was comforting. It was providential that Payton was driving the wagon. She'd have dissolved into uncontrollable sobbing if he had tried to console her.

They stopped when they reached El Puerto de Santa María and looked out over the wreckage of the abandoned French camp. "They didna take their siege gun with them, but they've made sure the Spaniards canna use it," Payton growled.

"Blown to bits," Kenneth agreed.

"Are they all like this?" Alba asked one of the guerrillas in the escort.

"No," he replied in the same language. "We captured many guns, thirty gunboats and a large quantity of equipment and provisions."

"Somehow," she confessed. "That makes me feel more optimistic."

They continued into the city itself. "Strangely deserted," Payton remarked.

"Siesta," Alba explained. "Nothing can deter Spaniards from observing age-old traditions."

Ballesteros had insisted it would be simple to arrange safe passage to Gibraltar, but Alba gaped when they reached the harbor. The port was crammed with ships flying the Royal Navy ensign.

Their escort led them to *HMS Valiant* and informed Alba that the vessel was due to leave for Gibraltar on the morrow.

"This doesna bode well," Payton said.

"Leave this to me," Kenneth declared.

~

KENNETH JUMPED down from the wagon and approached the *Valiant's* gangway. Two British marines barred his way. "I wish to see your captain," Kenneth explained.

"Captain's busy," came the reply from one.

"It's a matter of some urgency. Tell him the Duke of Ramsay must speak with him."

The smirking sailor looked him up and down before replying. "An' I spose he's brung the King wiv him."

This wasn't going to be as easy as Kenneth had assumed. Twice since leaving England, he'd bumped into former schoolmates. Most commissioned officers in the Royal Navy had at one time or another attended Eton or Harrow. He decided to take a chance. "Your captain will be annoyed if he finds out you've turned Kenny Hawkins away."

As he'd hoped, hesitation flickered in the sailor's eyes. He was instructed to wait while the second sailor conveyed the message.

Payton joined him on the dock. "What's happenin'?"

"Nothing, yet. I plan to use Prinny's name if my first ploy doesn't work."

The messenger returned. "Captain says he dinna ken Kenny Hawkins, so bugger off."

Payton stepped forward. "Is yer Captain a Scot as weel, laddie?"

The sailor smiled. "Aye. We're both from Inverness."

"Then, can I count on ye to tell yon Captain 'tis vital we get these barrels to the *Uachdaran* distillery in the Highlands."

"*Uachdaran?*"

"Aye."

"Finest bloody whisky to be found anywhere. Dinna fash, we'll get yon barrels loaded. Who's the lass?"

"An orphaned refugee," Kenneth replied.

Within minutes, Royal Navy ratings were carrying the barrels onto the man-o-war. One of Ballesteros' men drove away the empty wagon without a sound of protest from the mules. The sailor from Inverness escorted Kenneth, Payton and Alba up the gangway.

"Well done," Kenneth said to his cousin.

"We're just lucky the man was a Scot," Payton replied modestly.

"And a discerning whisky drinker."

"Aye."

WOMEN ARE FICKLE

"We've no agent in London, now," Tavish said as he and Niven made their way to the distillery early in the morning. "We dinna ken when or if Payton will return."

Niven was conflicted. He belonged in the Highlands, though his older brother didn't really need him now he had a larger workforce. In truth, he missed the busy activity in the Duke of Withenshawe's dockland offices. However, he was beginning to feel more comfortable with the idea of seriously wooing Daisy Hawkins. They'd attended a couple of barn dances together and he'd enjoyed her company. As was often the case, he'd been prevailed upon to play the fiddle, and she'd lavished praise on his prowess. He still wasn't sure, though, how she felt about living permanently in the Highlands. And, truth be told, he didn't find her sexually arousing. No matter how hard she tried to seduce him, his cock remained unenthusiastic. Perhaps if he took her to bed...

"Stop daydreaming and pay attention," Tavish

demanded. "Will ye go to London for a while? We canna expect Withenshawe to take care of our interests there. He has a shipping empire to run."

Still, Niven dithered. He often wished he had his brother's decisiveness, but perhaps that was the problem. Tavish had always made his decisions for him. Was that the reason he couldn't make up his mind about Daisy? A few weeks apart might clarify things. "Aye. I'll sail south from Dundee with the next shipment in two days."

"Good," his brother replied. "I'm confident I can depend on ye."

The unusual praise raised Niven's spirits. Tavish recognized he had been an effective agent in London, having rented a spacious warehouse and helped secure new markets. He could be just as useful to the distillery in England as he was in Glengeárr. In London, he seemed to have no trouble making decisions.

∼

DAISY FLUNG her hairbrush at Niven. It wasn't an effective weapon but it was all she had to hand. "You intend to leave me in this godforsaken place and hie off to London?" she screamed.

"Just for a wee while," he replied as he bent to retrieve the hairbrush from the floor. "I thought ye liked it here in Glengeárr."

"Oh, yes. I just love Uncle Gregor's scintillating company," she screeched. "Mama may like living in Lockie House, but the drafty place holds no appeal for me. And why would I want to attend balls and musicales when I can do the Barley Mow in a leaky barn and get my feet trodden on by some yokel."

"Is that what ye think o' me? A yokel."

Daisy took a deep breath. She'd gone too far and revealed too much. Scotland had only ever been a temporary inconvenience as far as she was concerned. "Of course not. I only came here to be with you and now you're leaving."

"I thought ye came to visit yer mother."

"That too. But she's in London now, as well. I want to go with you."

As usual, he dithered. She'd never met a man so incapable of making decisions. "It's settled, then," she declared. "When do we leave?"

~

Cat and Lady Maureen were sipping tea in the drawing room of the London Dower House. Cat had never acquired a taste for tea, but the English seemed to love it, so she went along with the twice-daily ritual. "Are you feeling more at home now you've been in London three weeks?" Kenneth's mother asked.

"Not at home precisely," she replied as honestly as she could. "But I feel I'm better dressed after our shopping expeditions and I'm grateful for the introductions ye've arranged."

"You're very tactful. That skill will stand you in good stead when you and Kenneth marry."

The knot in Cat's stomach tightened. They'd had no

word from Spain, except that the siege of Cádiz had been lifted. "I'm trying to keep my hopes in check," she confessed.

They were interrupted by the arrival of Lady Maureen's husband. She rose to accept his embrace. "I wasn't expecting you home from Withenshawe's offices for at least an hour."

"Weel," Sir Jock replied. "Ye willna credit who arrived with today's shipment o' whisky from Dundee."

Cat could think of only one person who'd be anxious to leave Glengeárr. Lady Maureen pursed her lips, evidently thinking along the same lines.

"I let them off at the main house," Jock said.

"Them?" Lady Maureen asked.

"Daisy and Niven."

Cat was surprised the two were still together. They didn't seem suited.

∽

It had taken seven days aboard ship with Niven to make Daisy realize she didn't love Niven. He was a nice man, kind and intelligent, but so indecisive. She needed a beau who took charge, preferably one who lived in London permanently.

Hoping he'd get the message, she'd thought the kindest thing was to avoid him, which she'd done for the past few days. Now, she stared at the engraved invitation in her hand. Since returning to London a week ago, she'd heard rumors, but here was the proof. Niven would have to be told about the invitation to Jasmine Foxworthy's wedding. She could scarcely believe the scatterbrain had managed to ensnare the Earl of Waterdown. Payton had been thrown over.

She waited up for Niven to arrive home from the Withenshawe offices. He smiled but wide eyes betrayed his surprise. A frown replaced the smile when she handed him the invitation. "This came today," she said.

She'd never seen Niven angry, but she saw it now as thunder darkened his handsome face.

He thrust the invitation back into her hands and growled, "Women are fickle creatures," before stomping up the stairs to his room. She was left with no doubt that part of his anger was justifiably directed at her.

~

Niven tossed and turned most of the night. Jasmine's betrayal rankled and he grieved for Payton's pain. He'd never liked the chit, nor understood what Payton saw in her, but his brother would be devastated.

The penniless nitwit had seduced an English earl and got him to the altar. Obviously, money and prestige carried more weight than her commitment to Payton.

His brother was selflessly risking his life for the benefit of the family distillery, but the courageous sacrifice clearly meant nothing to Miss Foxworthy.

As for his own treatment at Daisy's hands—what more was there to say?

It was never a good idea to trust a woman.

MI AMOR

The voyage from Cádiz to Gibraltar was a short one, just a few hours, but Alba spent as much time as she was allowed on the deck of *HMS Valiant*. Payton and Kenneth stood with her as they passed through the strait and she left her beloved Andalucía behind, probably never to return. The man she loved and his stalwart cousin seemed to sense she needed the silence as she entered a new world. Only the warm wind filling the sails spoke of change.

With Kenneth's assistance, she stepped off the man-o-war onto British soil—safe, but a refugee.

"I'll see to the unloading," Kenneth said before rushing away.

Payton pointed to a smaller vessel. "Yonder the *Matilda*, the schooner we arrived on."

She accepted his offer of escort and they walked arm in arm toward the ship he'd indicated. It felt so right to depend on his strong arm, to stroll along the dock as if they belonged together. He dwarfed her, but she'd never felt intimidated by his height. He could never be hers, but surely there was nothing amiss with accepting his protection. He would see her safely to Mull. The prospect was of no consolation for the loss of what might have been.

In contrast to their experience in Cádiz, the crew of the *Matilda* cheered when they caught sight of Payton. Kenneth's appearance in the company of a dozen Royal Navy ratings each rolling a barrel along the dock brought on more cheers and laughter.

A man who had the air of an officer approached. "I must admit I doubted you'd succeed," he exclaimed, shaking Payton's hand. "And who is this?"

"Captain Frame," Payton replied. "May I introduce *Señorita* Alba Castillero from Jerez. She'll be sailing with us."

The captain bowed courteously. "Welcome aboard," he declared, wiggling his eyebrows.

The knot of fear in her stomach loosened. She was not going to be denied permission to sail to England, but the captain evidently thought she was Payton's paramour.

"I'll send word to John Smith," Frame said. "He'll be delighted to hear you've completed your mission. I can't wait to learn how you managed to convince the Royal Navy to lend a hand."

"There are whisky connoisseurs everywhere, Captain. Even in the Royal Navy."

PAYTON AND THE PASSIONATE PARTISAN

PAYTON WAS ecstatic that he and Kenneth had accomplished the seemingly impossible task they'd set out to do. Tavish's long-held dream of aging *Uachdaran* whisky in wood permeated with sherry would come to fruition. It had been worth risking his life just to fulfill the dream of the brother he admired so much.

The barrels were tucked away in the ship's cargo hold. They'd taken advantage of the opportunity to bathe at Government House. His and Kenneth's own clothes had been retrieved. The Governor's wife had offered Alba one or two day dresses she no longer wore. They were too big on her, but she appreciated the gesture and insisted she felt better in clean clothing.

Payton and his cousin had survived unscathed, apart from a noticeable gash on Kenneth's temple. They'd become firm friends. However, a daunting voyage through difficult seas lay ahead. There was also the problem of Alba.

When Payton insisted that he and Kenneth intended to share a cabin and Alba would need her own, the bemused captain offered her his own accommodations.

As the ship cast off from Gibraltar, Payton looked his cousin in the eye. "I'd ask a favor o' ye."

"Of course."

"When we arrive in London, I'll seek out Jasmine and make arrangements for a quick wedding. I want you to take Alba to Ramsay House and arrange her journey to Mull."

"Won't you at least wait until we get home before you make a decision about your future?" Kenneth asked.

Payton shook his head. "The decision may ha'e been

hasty, but 'twas made long ago and now I must live with it."

~

"It's like sharing a cabin with a bad-tempered bear," Kenneth complained on the third afternoon at sea. It was obvious Payton and Alba cared deeply for each other, but Kenneth felt helpless to resolve the dilemma they faced.

"'Tis just my belly plaguing me," Payton replied. "Once we reach calmer waters..."

"It isn't seasickness, and you know it," Kenneth retorted. "Go and see her."

"Safer to stay here."

"Cruel more like it. The poor girl must be lonely and terrified of what lies ahead. She's lost everything near and dear to her. Talk to her about Scotland, about your distillery—anything. Be a man."

He braced himself for a retaliatory blow when his cousin clenched his fists but, apparently, the taunt did the trick. Payton left the cabin, slamming the door behind him.

Trying to ignore the pitching and rolling, Kenneth set his mind to the favor Payton had asked of him. He'd intended to go to Scotland as soon as possible to offer for Cat. Mull wasn't exactly on the way to the Highlands. Taking Alba there would be inconvenient but Mainwaring would figure out a way to kill two birds with one stone.

~

PAYTON AND THE PASSIONATE PARTISAN

Payton received no answer when he tapped on the cabin door. He put his ear to the metal, but heard nothing. He should walk away, punch Kenneth's nose then throw himself into the choppy waters of the Cantabrian Sea.

He didn't have the courage to do any of those things, so he eased open the door. "Alba," he said softly.

She lay curled up in the captain's berth.

Not wishing to startle her awake if she was sleeping, he stared at the woman who was in his blood. What was it about her that had him in her thrall? She was pretty, but he'd known women who were more beautiful. She had no breasts to speak of, but he thirsted to suckle her.

He tensed when she stirred. If he was quick about it, he could be out the door before...

"Payton?"

Too late.

Was it the soulful, tear-filled eyes, the quivering chin, or the exotic way she pronounced his name? Whatever the reason, his resolve flew out the window of the windowless cabin. He couldn't resist gathering her into his arms. "Alba, *mi amor*," he whispered.

FOR THE BEST

At Daisy's request, Niven agreed to accompany her to Jasmine's wedding. The prospect churned his belly, but he had to be there for Payton's sake.

Since they didn't know the bridegroom, they sat in the mostly empty pews on the bride's side of St. George's. Judging by the crowd of fashionably dressed folks on the Earl of Waterdown's side of the church, he was well known about town.

Beaming a broad smile, Foxworthy escorted his daughter down the aisle. Gowned in puffy layers of some filmy pink fabric, Jasmine was a vision of loveliness, though the breasts that had so enthralled Payton were on rather indecent display. The groom licked his lips as he watched his bride advance toward him.

"Stop grinding your teeth," Daisy hissed.

"Sorry. I'm just upset for my brother."

"You can't blame the chit," his cousin replied. "Payton could be dead for all we know."

Gooseflesh ran rampant up Niven's spine. Surely he'd have felt something if Payton had been killed? "I refuse to believe that," he growled. "He will return."

"I hope they both do," she replied sadly.

He'd been thoughtless. Of course she was worried for her own brother. "They'll have watched out for each other," he said, taking hold of her hand.

∼

JASMINE HADN'T REALIZED Niven King and Daisy Hawkins were present at her wedding until she was walking back down the aisle with her new husband. There were conflicting rumors about the pair, so she was surprised they were holding hands.

As usual, Daisy looked like she'd bitten into a whole lemon. It was clear from the stern set of Niven's jaw that he was angry. It was to be expected, she supposed, but she couldn't wait forever for Payton to return. Her mother had made her see that, and Justin was hard to resist. In fact, he could be downright domineering, especially in the bedroom. Heat flooded her face when she thought of the things they'd done together. Admittedly, she loved the orgasms, but the punishments when she came too soon not so much.

An enthusiastic crowd showered the newlyweds with rice outside the church. Jasmine wasn't surprised Niven and Daisy were not among them. She didn't like to think what might transpire if Payton did return. He'd be angry. It was as well Justin was whisking her off to his estate in Berkshire.

She was looking forward to seeing her new home where she could take up the mantle of Lady Jasmine Carmichael, Countess of Waterdown. That certainly sounded preferable to a future in the back of beyond as the wife of a Scottish whisky distiller.

～

Maureen invited her daughter and Niven to dinner. "I'm not sure what's going on between Daisy and the King boy," she confided to her husband. "Their relationship seems to be on one minute and off the next."

"However," Cat added. "Payton's brother will be justifiably upset about Jasmine's betrayal and 'tisna a good idea to brood alone on things."

"Aye," Jock replied. "When Kenneth returns, he'll be pleasantly surprised to find Cat here, whereas Payton..."

"Jilted for a richer prospect."

Voices in the foyer alerted everyone to the arrival of the guests and brought an end to the conversation. Nervous apprehension tightened Cat's throat. Since his return from Scotland, Niven had made no effort to come to the Dower House to see her. Did he blame her for this latest disappointment? It was true she and Payton had once been childhood sweethearts, but they'd both long since realized they weren't suited. Meeting Kenneth had opened Cat's eyes to what real love was.

Perhaps Niven thought it presumptuous of her to believe she was good enough to marry a duke.

All her misgivings went up in smoke when Niven entered the drawing room. They'd grown up together in a small, isolated village, played and teased with local lads and lasses. Their eyes met, each recognizing in the other a trusted friend from home.

"Cat," Niven exclaimed as he strode forward and embraced her. "'Tis good to see ye."

"Niven," she replied, feeling like a gust of fresh Highland air had just blown in. "I'm so sorry to hear about Payton's former fiancée."

"Weel," he replied. "I'm sure he'll be angry when he first learns o' Jasmine's treachery. No man likes to be thrown over for another. But, in the long run, I think 'tis for the best, and he'll eventually see that."

"And ye've heard naught from your brother, or Kenneth?" Cat asked, wishing she'd held her tongue.

"Nay," he replied with a sigh. "I watch the docks every day, hoping to see the *Matilda* return."

"Well, we just have to keep our hopes up," Kenneth's mother interjected. "I believe my son is still alive."

"I feel the same about Payton," Niven said.

Cat prayed they were both right.

"Let's go in to the dining room," Lady Maureen suggested.

Niven offered Cat his arm and escorted her to dinner.

Jock linked arms with his wife and a pouting Daisy.

⁓

As was often the case, Daisy felt like the odd one out. Throughout dinner, Cat and Niven chatted and laughed about people they knew in Glengeárr. They shared childhood memories. Niven's easy rapport with Cat confirmed

Daisy's growing belief that he wasn't the man for her and he knew it.

Her mother and Jock joined in, all the while exchanging loving glances. Daisy was certain they held hands under the table.

Even the horrid Jasmine had managed to marry a rich and handsome man.

She prayed desperately for Kenneth's safe return, but he'd be so taken with Cat when he came back, he'd have no time or inclination to set his mind to finding a match for his sister. If he and Payton had succeeded in retrieving the much-vaunted barrels, they'd be preoccupied with getting them to Scotland.

She was doomed to be the spinster aunt to her brother's children.

"Ye're quiet this evening," Jock remarked.

"Yes," her mother agreed. "Penny for your thoughts."

It was too much. Unwilling to explain a melancholy she didn't fully understand herself, she rose and left the dining room with a muttered, "Please excuse me."

CHANGE OF PLAN

Alba wished Payton would come to the cabin to comfort her, then, suddenly, she was in his arms and he was whispering endearments. Was it a dream? "Payton?" she asked again.

"Let me love ye, little warrior," he said as he lifted her.

Cradled in his embrace like a precious object, she knew he loved her. It was tempting to accept his love but he was promised to another. "What about your *prometida*?"

"I must be honest with ye. I dinna love Jasmine. I love ye. We can belong to each other for the short time we have left," he said. "Let me give ye pleasure. I willna dishonor ye."

Pleasure of any sort was something Alba hadn't experienced for a long time. Why not share kisses and more with her gentle Scot? She knew nothing of Mull nor her distant family there. Payton was the here and now.

He was offering his love and she craved him. "Aye," she whispered. "Kiss me."

He growled as his mouth took possession of hers. She willingly allowed his tongue entry and it seemed natural to suckle it greedily. She sifted her fingers through his hair. It was just as silky as she remembered from their first kiss. Before she had time to think, he'd easily settled them both in the berth without breaking the kiss. His big hands fumbled with the ties of her shirt. Impatient to reveal breasts she'd always considered inadequate, she pulled the shirt up and bared her body to his view.

He broke off the kiss, stared at her breasts for only a moment then bent his head to suckle a nipple.

A spasm of pleasure tore through her and blossomed in a very intimate place. "*Sí, sí,*" she cried, when he squeezed both nipples gently.

"*Mi tesoro,*" he rasped. "Can I taste ye?"

His meaning escaped her, but he didn't wait for an answer. He pushed her skirts to her waist and licked her nether lips. Soon, she was climbing a mountain of rapturous pleasure. He gripped her thighs with his powerful arms when she fell keening into an abyss of bliss.

~

PAYTON WAS IN TROUBLE. Alba's sweet taste on his lips had his greedy cock demanding more. But he couldn't take more, no matter how great the need to bury himself inside her.

With what little resolve he had left, he righted her

clothing and gathered her into his arms. She nuzzled her face into his chest, whispered *Te amo*, and was soon asleep.

Despite the turmoil in his loins, he was content to hold her, elated that she trusted him. He felt no guilt. He hadn't violated her nor betrayed his pledge to Jasmine. He'd pleasured a young woman he loved, without taking care of his own needs. What they'd shared was wholesome and right. Whatever the future held in store, he'd always have this memory to sustain him.

Eventually, the rocking movement of the ship lulled him to sleep.

There was very little light in the windowless cabin when he woke, so he had no idea how long he'd slept. He looked down at Alba. Wide eyes studied him. They gazed into each other's eyes for long minutes. Neither of them spoke but each felt the power of the silent message of love that passed between them.

~

KENNETH HAD his speech rehearsed when Payton returned to the cabin they shared. He'd lain awake most of the night weighing the pros and cons. "Listen," he began, suddenly doubting the wisdom of his thoughts.

"I'm nay in the mood for a lecture," his cousin replied.

"You're jumping to conclusions. I know exactly how it feels to love a woman you can't have. So, I have a plan."

"Aye. What is it?"

"Are you anxious to reunite with Jasmine?"

"Ye ken the answer to that question."

"Exactly. And I have decided to woo Catriona Neish until I convince her to be my duchess."

"I'm happy for ye, but I'm nay seein' the connection."

"Cat is in Scotland. I don't want to waste any more time as far as she is concerned. The barrels have to go to Scotland. If we sail there directly, you can spend more time with Alba. Tavish will be happy to get his sherry barrels sooner. Alba will have the chance to see the distillery for herself. From Glengeárr you can take her to Mull then eventually make your way to London and meet with Miss Foxworthy."

He stopped babbling. Payton was rubbing his chin, seemingly seeing the merit in what he'd proposed.

～

It was early afternoon when Payton and Kenneth both came to Alba's cabin. She was overjoyed to see Payton, but what did his cousin's presence mean? Could the man she loved not trust himself to be alone with her?

"We have news," Kenneth began. "There's been a change of plan."

She glanced quickly at Payton, but the stern set of his jaw made it hard to tell if he was happy with whatever changes were to take place. "Changes?"

"We willna be dockin' in London."

Relief flooded Alba's heart. Payton's betrothed was in London. "Where are we going?"

"Straight to Scotland," Kenneth replied. "First to Dundee, then overland to Glengeárr."

"This is so you can take the barrels directly to your brother's distillery?" she asked.

"Aye."

"And the captain is in agreement with this change?"

"He was reluctant initially," Kenneth confessed. "Until I pointed out that his employer and I are major investors in the Kings' distillery."

"And that ye're both dukes," Payton added with a chuckle.

"A duke?" Alba exclaimed. "*Duque?*"

Madre de dios, Kenneth was a duke!

"Yes," Kenneth admitted. "I didn't think it important to tell you. I went to Spain as a cousin and friend of the King brothers."

Alba wondered if there were perhaps things she didn't know about Payton.

"Before you ask," he said. "I'm nay a duke, just an ordinary man in love with an extraordinary woman."

She thought her heart might burst.

WHAT A COIL

Niven was saying goodnight to the employees at Withenshawe's London offices after another frustrating day of waiting for word of the *SS Matilda*. It was becoming increasingly difficult to concentrate on his duties. The longer the wait went on, the more certain he became that his brother and cousin were never coming back.

He startled when the duke himself burst into the office. "They've gone directly to Scotland," he exclaimed breathlessly.

Utter silence greeted this confusing news until the reality dawned on Niven. "They retrieved the barrels! They're alive!"

"It would seem so," Withenshawe replied with a smile. "Captain Frame put a man ashore at Southend with a message but, for some reason, it's taken him two days to get to London."

"There's many a pub on that road," someone shouted.

"They'll be well on their way to Dundee by now," Niven said, not caring if the fool had stopped in every pub on the way. His brother was alive. "I must let everyone at Ramsay House know."

"Just one other thing. The sailor reports an extra passenger on board."

"Another passenger?"

"A young Spanish woman, apparently."

Niven's spirits plunged. Payton would honor his pledge to Jasmine, though the fool didn't yet know of her treachery. Niven would have to tell Cat that Kenneth had brought home a Spanish lass.

~

CAT WAS DINING with Lady Maureen, Jock and Daisy when Niven rushed into the dining room of the Dower House. Flushed and breathless, he swallowed hard and declared, "They're alive. Kenneth and my brother are alive and well."

Jock jumped up from his chair and shook Niven's hand.

Lady Maureen burst into tears.

Laughing, Daisy threw herself into Niven's arms. Cat couldn't figure the woman out. Did she care for the man or not?

Cat wanted to laugh and cry too, but Niven seemed hesitant. And why hadn't Kenneth and Payton come home right away if they'd survived the adventure?

"Are they on the way here?" Lady Maureen asked.

"Nay," Niven replied, his brow furrowed.

"I suppose there's a lot to take care of," Jock suggested. "Unloading the barrels and so on. They did retrieve the barrels?"

"Aye."

Cat couldn't abide the suspense. "What is it ye're nay telling us?"

Niven swallowed hard. "They've sailed directly to Scotland."

A hush fell.

The turmoil in Cat's belly told her there was more to come.

"Makes sense," Jock finally said. "Seems a waste of time unloading them in London then loading them again."

Lady Maureen brightened. "Perhaps Kenneth decided to go to Scotland to see you, Cat."

Cat's doubts about that possibility were confirmed when Niven said, "They brought a Spanish woman with them."

Payton had no way of knowing about Jasmine's wedding so the woman must be with Kenneth. Cat's heart shattered.

~

MAUREEN LOOKED to her husband for inspiration. Jock always had the right answers. Now, he gaped like the rest of them, seemingly at a loss. "I'm sure there's some logical explanation," she tried.

"Logic dictates your son should marry someone of

his own class," Cat replied hoarsely. "This person must be a Spanish noblewoman."

That argument was valid, but Maureen refused to believe Cat's cause was lost. "Perhaps not. She might be a refugee, an orphan they took pity on."

"'Tis certainly possible," Niven said. "Payton and Kenneth are both generous and compassionate men who..."

Daisy interrupted. "A woman who travels alone with two men must be attached to one of them."

Not surprised when Cat fled the room in tears, Maureen collapsed into her chair. "When Kenneth reaches Glengeárr, he'll discover his family has decamped to London with Cat."

"Lord," Daisy exclaimed. "What a coil."

∽

"You mustn't give up hope," Daisy told Cat.

"'Twas hopeless right from the start," Cat replied, her sorrow muffled by the pillow. "I was a fool to believe yer brother loved me."

Feeling an uncharacteristic urge to console this woman she barely knew, Daisy perched on the edge of the bed and put a hand on Cat's back. "He does love you, I can attest to that. My brother is loyal to a fault. I can't believe he would wed someone else."

"But we made no promises one to the other," Cat wailed. "I must return to Scotland."

The possible ramifications of that made Daisy dizzy. What if Cat went to Scotland and Kenneth was indeed betrothed to this Spanish woman? "Er…no…I beg you to stay here until we know the facts. We might be jumping to the wrong conclusions."

"Ye're right. But I canna be here when Kenneth brings home his new love."

"But I think you'd be the person to console Payton when he returns and discovers Jasmine has wed another."

~

Cat had always been fond of Payton King. They'd grown up together in a small village, flirted with the notion of one day marrying and eventually become firm friends.

Their families had lived in the same glen for generations.

The prospect of consoling him held appeal, but also scared her to death. Throwing two broken-hearted people together might lead to…

No, she couldn't consider that possibility. Her feelings for Kenneth Hawkins were all-consuming. She had nothing but sympathy to offer Payton.

Lady Maureen might be reluctant to help plan a return journey to Scotland. The prospect of accomplishing such a thing herself was too daunting. She needed an ally.

~

Niven was more convinced than ever that this love business was something to be avoided. Cat had sacrificed everything to come to London, her love for Kenneth her only motivation. Now, she was in an untenable situation and there'd be nothing but tears and recrimination when Kenneth did eventually return with his Spanish conquest.

Niven's Aunty Maureen and her husband would be caught in the middle. They were firmly in Cat's camp, but would be obliged to welcome the Spaniard, especially if she and Kenneth did marry.

The laughable part was that Kenneth didn't even know he was breaking Cat's heart. He'd obviously tired of pining for her. Love simply didn't last.

DOUBTS CREEP IN

After a reasonably calm voyage, Alba stepped ashore on Scottish soil. Dundee was far from Mull, but it was still the land of her mother's birth. She filled her lungs with the chilly air, trying not to think about the daunting challenges this new beginning would bring. The reek of fish brought strange comfort. It reminded her of Cádiz. Though it was still early morning, the port was busy with men rushing here and there. The bearded, sweating workers could be Spaniards, except she didn't understand a word of what they were shouting to each other.

But Scotland also signaled an end to the pleasures she and Payton had shared on board ship—pleasures that had transformed her from a girl into a woman. She was still a maiden in fact, though not in her heart.

Kenneth was so intent on reuniting with a woman named Catriona, Alba suspected he either hadn't paid attention to Payton's absence from their cabin, or he approved of the time they spent together.

Captain Frame soon had the barrels loaded onto a wagon he commandeered. It was clear he held sway among the dockworkers, all of whom apparently worked for the Duke of Withenshawe. Her traveling companions had mentioned this rich duke but Kenneth preempted any questions she thought to pose.

"I canna wait to see Cat," he gushed.

Payton chuckled. "Ye're suddenly talkin' like a Scot, Cousin."

"Aye. This country is definitely in my blood."

Kenneth had mentioned his mother was a Scot. Scottish blood ran in Alba's veins, but did that mean she would eventually feel at home here? "How far is it to Glengeárr?" she asked nervously.

"We should be there by tomorrow night," Payton replied.

Alba eyed the wagon. In Spain, she'd walked for miles and sometimes ridden a mule, but the wagon didn't look very comfortable and the barrels took up most of the space.

Payton put his arm around her waist. "Dinna fash. Frame has organized a carriage for us, and we'll stay o'ernight at an inn on the way."

"That is good news, but what does *fash* mean?"

"It means don't worry, don't let it bother you," Kenneth explained.

Alba nodded. She wouldn't *fash* until the time came to say farewell to Payton.

~

PAYTON AND THE PASSIONATE PARTISAN

THE WAGON MOVED at a snail's pace and the carriage driver kept his team in check so as not to get too far ahead. Kenneth talked incessantly about Cat and his plans to get her to London. He sought Payton's opinion as to whether they should marry in Scotland. Cooped up with a woman he craved but couldn't touch, Payton feared he might go mad—or murder his cousin.

Pleasuring each other had been a mistake. He couldn't get Alba's sweet taste out of his mouth. Every bump in the road wafted her unique scent into his nostrils and stirred renewed interest in his manhood, just when he thought he had his urges under control.

Alba sat in one corner of the carriage, her attention seemingly fixed on the passing scenery. He avoided looking at her lest he fall on her like a hungry beast.

An argument broke out when they stopped overnight at the inn. The landlord at first refused to rent rooms to three dusty travelers—two unmarried men traveling with a woman. Blushing profusely, Alba fidgeted, clearly embarrassed by the situation. Payton was ready to punch the fool in the nose when Kenneth played the ducal card. The innkeeper only accepted this assertion when the carriage driver verified his passenger's identity.

"I hope tomorrow won't be as stressful as today," a fuming Kenneth exclaimed when he and Payton were settling into their room.

Payton agreed but, to his way of thinking, his cousin was the source of the stress. "Mayhap if ye stop goin' on about Catriona Neish."

Kenneth paused in unpacking his valise. "I suppose you're right. However, put Alba out of her misery and hold her. She needs your reassurance that all will be well in this new country."

Hopelessness swept over Payton. "How can all be well when we love each other but I must marry another?"

Kenneth tested the mattress. "For a long while, that was my reasoning. But I was wrong. You need to think seriously about your commitment to Jasmine."

"I've thought of naught else."

"If you insist on marrying Miss Foxworthy, you're condemning her and yourself to lifelong unhappiness."

His words were a blow to the belly. Payton's parents hadn't loved each other. The lack of affection had eventually turned them into bitter people who took their resentment out on their three sons until Tavish was old enough to protect his younger brothers from the beatings. Marrying Jasmine was a bleak prospect, especially since his heart knew she would never consent to live in Scotland. "Ye're right. I've some thinkin' to do."

"Meanwhile, enjoy the time you have left with Alba."

"Aye. Nay tonight, though. Yon innkeeper has threatened us wi' death if either of us so much as goes near her room."

～

KENNETH COULDN'T SLEEP, partly because Payton spent half the night pacing back and forth, but mostly thanks to a vague sense of unease about his reception in Glengeárr. All these months, he'd believed Cat loved him, but what if she didn't? He'd based his belief on one incendiary farewell kiss. Perhaps that was folly.

If she rejected his proposal, he'd have to stay with his mother at Lockie House and lick his wounds. The prospect left a bitter taste in his mouth.

"Try to get some sleep," he finally pleaded.

Payton grunted something unintelligible, but he stopped pacing and got into bed.

Kenneth wasn't certain how much time had crawled by when Payton asked, "Are ye asleep?"

"No."

"I just want to thank ye for yer help in Spain. Nay matter where life takes us, I hope we can remain friends."

"You can count on it, Payton. I'm glad I came with you. I consider you the brother I never had."

REUNION

Tavish King happened to be leaving the distillery after a long but rewarding day when he espied a wagon approaching in the distance. He didn't immediately recognize the driver, nor the drayhorse pulling the wagon. However, there was no mistaking the cargo. Barrels.

He'd reluctantly given up hope of Payton and Kenneth's foray into Spain bearing fruit, so he quashed the faint hope that insisted on entering his heart. He'd almost reconciled himself to Payton's death, although he'd never be able to fully accept the loss of his brother unless he saw a body. The possibility Payton lay cold and dead in some faraway unmarked grave couldn't be borne. The worst of it was, he knew only too well that Payton had undertaken the journey to please him.

"Ye and yer foolish ideas, Tavish King," he exclaimed to the gathering shadows. "Aging whisky in sherry barrels."

He swallowed the lump in his throat when he

noticed there was a carriage following the wagon. Narrowing his eyes, he could see it was one of Withenshawe's vehicles—and someone was leaning out of the window, waving.

Payton?

Could it be?

What began as an optimistic jog turned into a full-blown sprint when he realized it was indeed his brother waving and yelling. Payton leaped from the carriage into Tavish's arms. Thumping each other on the back, they let the tears of joy fall unashamedly.

When Tavish was able to breathe again, he was equally glad to see Kenneth emerge. "Ye both survived, and ye brought the barrels."

"Aye," Payton confirmed, turning to assist a diminutive young woman. "And 'tisna all we brought from Spain. Alba, I'd like ye to meet my brother, Tavish. He's the master distiller."

The lass's skin and hair coloring put Tavish in mind of Cat Neish, so he wondered whose companion she was. "Welcome, Alba. Ye look like a Spaniard but ye've a Scottish name."

"Aye, Tavish," she replied. "My mother was a Scot, from Mull."

Payton's smile fled. "And I'll be taking her there once Kenneth settles things wi' Cat."

Tavish was confused. "Cat? Did ye nay see her in London?"

~

PIPER KING WAS STIRRING a large pot of stew bubbling on the wood-stove when her husband burst into the kitchen. It took her a moment to realize the identities of the bearded men with Tavish. "Payton," she exclaimed as she dropped the wooden spoon and rushed into her brother-in-law's embrace. "Thank God."

"And look who's with him," Tavish said, as if she hadn't recognized the duke who'd once tried to woo her. She was relieved to see him alive and well but would her husband consider it inappropriate for her to hug him? "Kenneth, I'm so happy ye've returned safely."

"Give him a hug, Piper," Tavish said. "He's had some bad news."

Before she could ask, a petite young woman appeared from behind Payton's back. "I'm Alba Castillero," she said with a trace of a foreign accent.

"'Twas her family's sherry distillery that received our barrel staves," Tavish explained.

"I'm pleased to meet ye, Alba," Piper said. "Though I'm nay understandin'."

"Listen to you," Kenneth quipped, pecking a kiss on her cheek. "Ye sound like a Scot."

"The accent's infectious," Piper replied. "Ye live wi' Scots, ye canna help but start to speak like a Scot. Now, can somebody explain all this?"

∼

KENNETH'S EMOTIONS were all over the place as he sat down to enjoy a hearty meal in Tavish's comfortable home. "I was utterly disappointed to learn Cat isn't in Glengeárr," he confessed.

"But she went to London to be with ye," Tavish replied.

"And, fool that I am, I went off to Spain."

"She must be waiting anxiously for news," Piper said.

Payton chuckled. "Ironically, 'twas our cousin's idea for the ship to bypass London, he was in such a rush to get here."

"I had a suspicion my mother was plotting something to get me and Cat together. I admit I am astonished to hear Daisy came to Scotland. With Niven of all people?"

"That's a whole other story," Piper exclaimed. "It's an on-again-off-again romance."

"Daisy worries me," Kenneth admitted. "Still, one day she'll perhaps meet someone who'll knock her off her feet, so to speak. Like with me and Cat."

"Do you really regret going to Spain?" Alba asked quietly.

"Heavens, no," Kenneth replied, not wishing to dredge up the horrors they'd seen. There'd be time enough for that. "Payton and I had a marvelous adventure and became firm friends. Plus, we met you and your father and were able to bring you to safety here."

"So," Piper said hesitantly. "Ye'll be off to London to propose to Cat, and Payton intends to take Alba to Mull?"

"Her mother's family is there," Payton replied without enthusiasm. "I promised to see her safely delivered."

Kenneth was disappointed his cousin apparently still

intended to forsake the woman he loved and marry Jasmine.

∽

It was decided Payton and Kenneth would stay at another house that belonged to Kenneth's mother. Messages were sent to the servants to prepare rooms. Piper apparently sensed Alba's exhaustion and suggested she show her guest to a bedroom. In the meantime, the men sat downstairs talking. Tavish had asked for an account of the Spanish adventure.

Alba could hear their muffled voices as she lay awake in the bedroom Piper told her once belonged to Payton. So much had happened in the past few days, it was difficult to stop the thoughts colliding with each other in her brain.

She wondered what explanation Payton would give for her flight from Spain and his determination to take her to Mull. What would her rescuers tell Tavish about the ruined *bodega*? Would he admit that he loved her?

She buried her face in the pillow to muffle the sobs. She resolved to harden herself. Crying and worrying about things over which she had no control would only lead to further heartbreak. Payton might never share her bed again, but at least she was sleeping in the room where he'd slept for years. Alba the warrior had to be content with that.

∽

Tavish listened, enthralled by the harrowing tale told by his brother and cousin. "I wish I could visit the *bodega*," he said. "The system of stacking the barrels sounds intriguing."

"The war will be over one day. Alba can probably tell ye more about the process o' making fine sherry," Payton replied.

During the telling of the adventure, Tavish noticed his brother's uncharacteristically subdued manner, whereas Kenneth's recounting brought the events to life. "Ye say one o' the barrels is still full o sherry?" he asked, hoping to lift his brother's spirits. "I canna wait to taste it."

"Mayhap before I leave," Kenneth suggested.

"Aye. We'll tap it on the morrow."

The comfortable silence lengthened as Tavish thought about what he had learned of Spain, of sherry and of the two men who sat sipping whisky with him now. "Ye have become friends," he finally said.

It was a short while before Kenneth replied. "When you face death with a man, he becomes more than a friend. Payton and I will share that bond as long as we live."

"Aye," Payton echoed.

An unreasonable pang of jealousy tightened Tavish's throat. Payton was *his* brother—but it was true their lives had gone separate ways. Tavish had his darling Piper and his successful distillery. He wondered what lay in store for his brother. It was painfully clear Payton and the Spanish lass were in love with each other. Tavish remembered Jasmine Foxworthy and had never understood what Payton saw in her—apart from the obvious.

When Payton and Kenneth left for Lockie House, Tavish climbed the stairs to his bedroom, stripped off his clothes, stared at his sleeping son for a minute or two, then slipped into bed.

"You're cold," Piper complained.

"Ye'll soon warm me up," he replied, cuddling into her naked body.

"Do ye think Payton truly intends to take Alba to Mull?" she asked.

"Ye sensed it too?" he replied.

"He loves her."

"Aye," he sighed, thankful for a life of contentment with the woman he loved.

ALBA TOURS THE DISTILLERY

"You are very kind to welcome me into your home," Alba told Piper as they ate breakfast together. "What is it we are eating?"

Piper chuckled. "Porridge oats. Highlanders must have it for their breakfast."

"It's hearty and delicious, and you have been so generous to give me some of your clothing."

"You're smaller than I am, but we'll soon make them fit. I brought a lot of my wardrobe with me from London but, to be honest, I never wear most of it here."

"Still, I am grateful."

"We are happy to have you as our guest," Piper replied. "I can't imagine the horrors you faced in Spain. You can stay here as long as you wish."

Alba suspected Piper would be truly horrified if she learned of the atrocities committed by both sides in the war. "Someday, maybe I will be able to talk about the invasion, but not yet."

"Of course. Payton explained your father is still fighting the French."

"Yes. He will never leave Spain."

"But he wanted you to be safe."

"With my aunt in Mull."

"Are you looking forward to meeting your Scottish family?"

Alba detected more than simple curiosity in the question. "I would like to meet my relatives..."

"But you'd prefer to stay here...with Payton."

"I don't hide my feelings very well, do I?"

"Neither does my brother-in-law. It's obvious he cares for you."

"But we have no future if he is to wed this Jasmine person."

"I've met Jasmine. She's flighty."

"What does this mean—flighty?"

"It means I doubt she is being as faithful to Payton as he insists on being to her."

Alba pondered Piper's words. If Jasmine had broken her promise to Payton...

Her musing was interrupted by Payton's arrival. She had only to see him again to confirm what her heart knew—she loved him. The sooner she left the Highlands, the better. Being close to the man she loved but couldn't have was torture. The improbable suggestion that Jasmine may have deserted him only made matters worse. Surely the woman knew what a prize she had in her grasp?

They gazed into each other's eyes for long minutes

until Payton grinned and asked, "Ready for yer tour o' the distillery?"

~

His brothers acknowledged Tavish as the master distiller. Payton and Niven were extremely proud of the successful enterprise they'd helped build, but it was Tavish's vision and creativity that had produced *Uachdaran*, a single malt so fine the Regent had granted a royal warrant.

Payton therefore appreciated Tavish keeping to the background and allowing him to explain the process to Alba as they strolled through the distillery.

She listened intently and asked intelligent questions. She remarked on the similarities and differences between distilling whisky and producing sherry. Tavish was clearly impressed and in turn asked her about the workings of the *bodega* she'd left behind.

"Time to tap the sherry barrel," Tavish declared when the tour wound up sampling whisky in the cellar.

"I second that," Kenneth said as he joined them.

"First," Alba replied. "I still have the taste of your fine whisky in my mouth. Can we have water before you sample my sherry?"

"I'll fill a jug at the pump," Kenneth said as he left.

Payton chuckled. Having politely sipped her first taste of whisky, Alba had tried hard not to grimace. "'Tis an acquired taste," he whispered close to her ear while they waited.

"A beverage more suited to men, I think," she giggled with a wink, aggravating his craving to make her his.

"Dinna suggest that to the auld women hereabouts," he replied.

She laughed out loud, worsening the uproar in his balls. It occurred to him he'd never heard Jasmine laugh. His fiancée always seemed incapable of seeing the humor in anything he said. It sounded a death knell for a man who always had a witty pun or two up his sleeve.

∽

After sampling Alba's fine sherry, Tavish considered the first step in making use of the new barrels. "We should drain the small amounts of sherry *Señor* Castillero left in each barrel, then transfer some *Uachdaran* into the barrels from Spain. We canna risk letting them dry out."

The process of draining the sherry and adding it to the fuller barrel didn't take long. Tavish was impressed that Alba insisted on helping the men. She was clearly familiar with tapping and filling barrels.

They were about to start transferring some of the year-old whisky into the sherry barrels when Piper arrived. "I thought we could make a start on altering the outfits you chose, Alba," she said.

Alba agreed but wanted to stay to watch the first of her barrels being filled with *Uachdaran*.

Holding back welling tears when the process was complete, she went willingly into Payton's outstretched arms.

"*Gracias*, Alba," he said hoarsely before handing her over to Piper.

"Yes, a thousand thanks," Kenneth echoed, shaking Payton's hand. "We did it, old chap."

"Aye," Tavish said hoarsely after the women had left. "And ye're a bluidy fool if ye let that woman go, Payton."

"So, Tavish," his brother replied. "Are ye happy now yer dream has come true?"

"Dinna change the subject. Alba belongs here, with ye."

"I keep telling him that," Kenneth said. "He's determined to honor his commitment to Miss Foxworthy."

"I promised Pedro I'd take her to Mull," Payton retorted.

"I met Castillero," Kenneth said. "I'd wager he'd be happy knowing his daughter had settled down with a whisky distiller she loves," Kenneth said. "It's why he suggested she come with us in the first place, and you know it."

"In any case," Tavish added. "'Tis too late in the year to think about venturing to Mull. Ye'd risk getting trapped by a blizzard in the Grampians."

THE LETTER

Over the course of the following week, Payton began to dread the dawning of each new day that signaled the rapid approach of Kenneth's imminent departure from Scotland.

Tavish and Kenneth kept hounding him to write a letter to Jasmine, canceling their betrothal. Kenneth had offered to deliver the letter when he got to London.

It was the coward's way out as far as Payton was concerned. Seeing Alba every day only added to his turmoil. Watching her become familiar with the distillery that meant so much to him was gratifying but heart-wrenching. The people of Glengeárr had taken a liking to her, and she to them. She'd be heartbroken when the time came to leave.

They couldn't indulge in any activity that might suggest a relationship. The abstinence was killing him, but Uncle Gregor would flay him alive if he so much as kissed Alba. His brother and cousin were irritatingly right. She was perfect for him and well suited to life in Scotland. Scottish blood ran in her veins. She was courageous and hardy. Her knowledge and experience would make her an asset to the distillery.

Tavish was correct when he warned of the dangers of traveling to Mull so late in the year. Payton couldn't expose Alba to the possibility of freezing to death in the mountains. She'd endured too much danger already. However, he might go mad if they had to spend the long winter months together in Glengeárr.

At the last possible moment, he penned a letter, but only to explain he'd been delayed in Scotland and would come to London as soon as possible.

Obviously assuming the letter canceled the betrothal, Kenneth accepted it with a grin and slapped him on the back. "You're doing the right thing," his cousin said.

Payton cringed. He no longer had any idea what the right thing was.

~

IT PAINED Alba to see Kenneth leave. She respected and liked the English nobleman alongside whom she had faced impossible odds. He had become a dear friend and she would miss him. "I wish you well in pursuit of the woman you so obviously love," she told him.

"And I'm confident all will turn out well for you too," he replied, patting the breast pocket of his topcoat. His wink only served to increase her confusion.

She was aware Payton's brother and cousin had implored him to write to Jasmine. Was Kenneth the bearer of such a letter? If so, what were the contents of the missive? He'd told her nothing. The stern set of his jaw betrayed his reluctance to say goodbye to Kenneth which made this an inopportune moment to confront him.

The journey to Mull had been postponed. She was glad of it. She'd never seen snow but trusted the dire warnings about blizzards in the mountains. She was assured by everyone she met that there'd be time enough to experience snow in Glengeárr.

She liked living without the constant threat of danger. Staying longer meant more time with her friend Piper King, and more opportunity to help in the distillery. Tavish had shown her how to update the ledgers, a task he was anxious to delegate, having apparently taken it on after Cat's departure.

When the *bodega* was flourishing, she'd helped her mother with a similar responsibility. Here she tallied barley, not grapes, shipments and sales of whisky, not sherry.

In theory, there was enough to see and do in Glengeárr to take her mind off Payton and her longing to make him hers. Unfortunately, nothing worked to lessen her frustration.

~

IN DUNDEE, Kenneth supervised the loading of a dozen barrels of *Uachdaran* into the hold of a Withenshawe ship, then boarded. He was greeted by the Captain with the respect due his title and shown to a comfortable cabin.

After a day and a half on the road from Glengeárr, he was ready for a nap. He removed his topcoat and climbed into his bunk.

Hands behind his head and ankles crossed, he contemplated the events of the past few months. To all intents and purposes, he was back to being the Duke of Ramsay, but Spain had been a life-altering experience. From now on, he resolved to be a different kind of duke, one more focussed on the important things in life rather than snobbish expectations and the useless perks of wealth and position. Fewer balls, nights of playing cards and time-wasting rides through Hyde Park just to be seen. More involvement in good works and the needs of his tenants. Perhaps even a foray into local government and better attendance in the Lords.

Kenneth was confident the Spanish partisans and the coalition forces would one day oust Napoleon from Spain. The tide had already turned with the failure of the siege of Cádiz. It wasn't beyond the realm of possibility that Bonaparte would then turn his greedy attention to invading England in retribution. Kenneth liked to think he would resist such an attack with as much courage and determination as the Castilleros and their comrades.

What a passionate warrior Alba had turned out to be. Payton was a fool if he abandoned her. She was a strong woman, not like Jasmine.

Thinking of strong women brought his thoughts back to Cat. He couldn't wait to be reunited with her. Her move to London indicated a wish to be with him. He was so convinced of the rightness of marrying her, he'd written to Mainwaring instructing him to procure a special marriage license.

When the ship's movement signaled the start of the voyage, he glanced across at his topcoat thrown carelessly onto the back of a chair. Payton's letter was in the inside pocket. He'd promised to deliver it, but wished he was sure of the contents. He could always open it then put it in another envelope once he got home. If Payton didn't have the gumption to get rid of the unsuitable chit, perhaps it was up to the Duke of Ramsay.

DOCKLAND CONFRONTATION

Her stomach in knots, Cat waited for Lady Maureen's return to the Dower House. Her patroness had gone to the main house with her husband. Tired of waiting for news from Scotland, they intended to interrogate Kenneth's man of business to ascertain if he had received any word.

Steeling herself for bad news, Cat gripped the edge of the settee when an unsmiling Lady Maureen entered the drawing room.

"Mainwaring has indeed received a letter from my son. He is probably on his way home as we speak."

This was good news, so why the stern set of Lady Maureen's jaw?

"It's rather confusing. Kenneth has instructed Mainwaring to procure a special license."

"A license for what?" Cat asked. Things always seemed so complicated here in England.

"A special license makes a quick wedding possible."

Cat's hopes and dreams flew out of the window. "He plans to wed the Spanish woman."

"Not necessarily. Forgive the comparison but Mainwaring was like the cat who swallowed the cream. He coyly refused to provide more details. Jock is still badgering him. We'll know more when Kenneth gets here."

Cat didn't need to hear more. She couldn't bear the prospect of seeing Kenneth with another woman. With Niven's help, she'd hatched a secret plan to sail back to Scotland on the next ship to leave for Dundee.

∼

"I can't wait about all day," the hackney driver groused. "Is yer lady-love coming or not?"

"She's nay my lady-love," Niven protested, nervous about having the hackney hang about outside Ramsay House. The same driver came to pick him up every day of the week. Usually, they were off straightaway to the Duke of Withenshawe's dockland offices. Today, he'd instructed the fellow to wait. Cat planned to walk the half mile from the Dower House and make her escape in the cab.

It saddened Niven that the romance between Cat and his cousin seemed to be over but, given his own experience in affairs of the heart, he supposed he shouldn't be surprised. Cat was adamant she wanted to go home to Glengeárr and she'd turned to him as an ally. What else could he do but help her? His Aunty Maureen wouldn't be pleased, but Cat's wellbeing came first. He'd known her all his life.

He stopped chewing his nails when she emerged from the pre-dawn shadows. Smiling his encouragement, he took her valise, helped her board and they were off. A half hour later, they'd crossed London and entered the seedy dockland area. Cat hadn't said a word. She'd simply stared out the window, though he doubted she'd even noticed it had grown lighter.

Withenshawe's navvies working on the dock informed them the ship Cat was to board had been delayed by a storm off the Norfolk coast. When it arrived, it would take a good while to unload the cargo. Cat stared into nothingness, seemingly in a trance after receiving this news. Concerned, Niven therefore escorted her into the offices, hoping there was someone available to make tea.

∼

KENNETH WAS RUNNING out of patience. The voyage from Dundee seemed endless enough without the ship's arrival in London being delayed by a storm. If he didn't get to hold Cat in his arms soon, he feared his heart might burst. Supervising the unloading of the latest shipment of *Uachdaran* would take time, unless he could find someone else to do it.

As the ship pulled into the dock, he was relieved to see Niven King on the wharf. Surely his cousin wouldn't mind taking over the duty. He waved to attract Niven's attention. To his great astonishment, his cousin turned tail and ran off into the offices when he saw him.

Irritated, he strode down the gangway when the captain gave the all clear to disembark. Fully intending to give Niven a piece of his mind, he made for the offices in the hope of finding someone to supervise the unloading.

He forced himself to count to ten when Niven blocked his way at the entry door. "What is wrong with you? Let me pass," he finally growled.

"I canna allow ye to go in," Niven insisted, fists raised.

"Have you lost your mind, Cousin?"

"There's someone inside who doesna wish to see ye and yer Spanish woman."

"My Spanish woman?" Kenneth asked, totally perplexed. Then—"Oh, you must mean Alba Castillero."

"Whatever her name, she isna...is she still aboard?"

The fog was starting to lift from Kenneth's brain. "Alba is still in Scotland."

"So, I suppose she'll be joinin' ye later?"

"I doubt it. It's my hope she'll be marrying Payton, if I can dissuade Jasmine..."

Niven relaxed his fists. "Ye mean to tell me the Spaniard and Payton..."

"Aye! They love each other. But your brother is being stubborn. He thinks he should honor his promises to Miss Foxworthy."

"But Jasmine married someone else—a rich earl."

The news took Kenneth so completely by surprise, he laughed out loud, but then he recalled what Niven had said. Someone was inside who definitely did not want to see Kenneth because she thought he was in love with a Spanish woman. "Cat is here?" he asked, deafened by the beating of his own heart.

Not willing to wait for the obvious answer, he shoved Niven aside in his haste to take the stairs up to the offices.

∽

STILL HOLDING the cup of tea she hadn't wanted in the first place, Cat caught sight of Kenneth on the ship's deck. Niven had obviously seen him too, hence his rush to get inside and let her know.

"He canna see me here," she murmured to Niven, thrusting the teacup and saucer at him.

"I'll stop him," Niven assured her, passing the cold tea to a puzzled employee of the shipping line.

Casting about desperately for a place to hide, Cat wondered idly what had become of the Spanish woman.

Suddenly, Kenneth burst through the door.

She backed away, her heart breaking for what might have been.

His hungry perusal confused her, as did the speed with which he crossed the room and took her into his embrace. "My darling Cat, I cannot tell you how much I have missed you."

The gall of the man, feigning affection when she knew for a fact he'd brought home a Spanish woman. The temptation to melt into his strong body was powerful, but she resisted.

Then he was down on one knee. "I don't blame you for being upset when you discovered I'd gone off to Spain. But I'm here now and I want you to be my wife. Mainwaring has hopefully procured the special license so we can marry soon."

"The special license is so you can marry me?" she asked, dumbfounded by what was happening. "But what about...?

"'Tis Payton who is in love with the Spaniard," Niven yelled as he too burst into the office.

The *ton* considered it bad form for a lady to throw herself at a man, but Cat didn't care what people thought. She stood on tiptoe and kissed Kenneth on the lips. She suckled his tongue when he deepened the kiss, inhaling the long-remembered scent of his skin.

Whistling broke them apart.

"I assume you accept my proposal?" Kenneth asked, brows arched. "Or will it take another kiss to persuade you?"

"I'm sure 'twillna be necessary," Niven quipped. "Else the two o' ye set the offices afire."

Bubbling with unexpected happiness, Cat recalled what Niven had said about his brother. "So, does Payton know about Jasmine?"

SOLUTIONS

Lost in thoughts of what might have become of the missing Cat, Lady Maureen was distracted by a noisy commotion in the foyer.

Her husband had been sitting with legs spread, arms resting on his thighs, head bent. Now, Jock perked up and looked to the door. "Sounds like Kenneth."

Daisy leaped up from the settee.

Maureen's heart threatened to burst when her son walked into the drawing room, Cat in tow. Both looked very happy. Evidently, the problem of the Spanish woman had been resolved.

Maureen was on her feet in a trice anxious to welcome her prodigal son into her open arms. "Kenneth, my dear boy," she said hoarsely as he hugged her. "What a relief."

"And I'm relieved to be home," he replied. "I have to apologize to everyone for the misunderstanding about Alba."

"Alba?" Jock asked, shaking Kenneth's hand.

"She's a Spanish woman, a member of the people's army that's giving Napoleon a run for his money."

"I heard something of the kind," Jock said.

"Her father asked us to bring her to safety. Her mother was Scottish and Alba has relatives in Mull. It turned out her father's vineyard was where the Kings sent their barrel staves years ago."

"So, where is she now?" Daisy asked.

"In Glengeárr, with Payton, which is where I hope she'll stay."

The reality of the situation was beginning to dawn on Maureen. "Payton doesn't know about Jasmine, does he?"

"No," Kenneth confirmed. "I thought I had convinced him to cancel the betrothal in a letter. He did write, but only to tell Jasmine he'd been delayed by winter weather and would return to London as soon as possible. I confess I opened the letter and read it."

"Given Jasmine's betrayal, it's a good thing you did," Daisy said.

Jock smiled. "And you think Payton and Alba..."

"Made for each other," Kenneth replied with a wink. "Like Cat and a certain duke."

Maureen's hopes rose. "Does this mean...?

"I'm honored to tell you Cat has agreed to be my duchess."

So much hugging, kissing and crying went on following this announcement, no one paid attention when Niven came quietly into the room—until he cleared his throat.

"Niven," Maureen exclaimed. "Isn't this wonderful news?"

"Aye," he replied, a twinkle in his eye as he bestowed a courtly kiss on Cat's knuckles.

"I suppose I'll have to get used to such courtesies," a blushing Cat said. "But how are we going to let Payton know about Jasmine?"

"Leave that to me," Niven replied, easing Maureen's concerns about her nephew. "As his brother, 'tis my responsibility to tell him."

~

ALBA HADN'T KNOWN either of her grandfathers. One had died before she was born and her Scottish grandsire lived far away from Spain—if he were even still alive.

Hence, she enjoyed conversations with Payton's Uncle Gregor. Everyone said he was a crusty old man, but Alba found his rambling tales fascinating. She learned a great deal about Scotland's troubled history. Spending time with him provided a respite from the temptation of Payton.

For a man who'd apparently only ever traveled beyond Glengeárr once, Gregor knew a lot about the isles off the west coast. He regaled her with tales of Mull. He even knew of the shipwreck that her family believed had resulted in the deaths of her ancestors.

"You make me eager to see Mull for myself," she admitted. "I suppose once the winter is over..."

"Aye," he said. "Though yer Spanish ancestors didna reach the west coast by traversing the mountains."

"Oh?" she replied. If there was a way to escape the temptation of Payton sooner, she'd reluctantly take it.

"Ye ken the Armada was blown into the North Sea after the defeat at Gravelines?"

"Aye," she replied.

"Unable to retrace his route through the Channel, the Spanish commander was forced to order his fleet to sail for home round the northern tip of Scotland and down the west coast of Ireland. 'Twas a daunting prospect for a fleet short of food and water, with many of the ships severely battle damaged and unsuited for such inhospitable waters. 'Tis said the storms were unusually fierce that year. They didna have charts and 'tis the reason many ended up sailin' along Scotland's west coast instead of Ireland."

She'd known most of the tragic details he recounted, but the reminder of the tale offered a possibility. "Do you think today's modern ships could make such a voyage?" she asked.

"Oh, aye. There's vessels leave Edinburgh that sail the northern route to the Isles."

A plan began to form in Alba's mind. If she devised a way to get to Edinburgh, she could take ship for Mull and escape the torment of living close to a man she couldn't have.

"The lads and I once stayed at a fine inn called *The White Horse* but we didna care much for Edinburgh," he added. "Folk there dinna wear the kilt. Tavish sends a man once in a while to fetch more *Uachdaran* bottles from our supplier."

He carried on the tale of the inn in Edinburgh being

named for the favorite steed of Mary, Queen of Scots, but Alba's thoughts were occupied elsewhere.

∾

THE OLD KENNETH HAWKINS, Duke of Ramsay, would have insisted on being married in London's most suitable society church with as many members of the English nobility in attendance as possible.

Pledging himself to Catriona Neish in the drawing room of his home felt more than right to the new Kenneth Hawkins. People he loved were present—his mother and Jock, his sister, and Niven King. Niven acted as his best man. Kenneth would have preferred Payton do the honors, but that wasn't possible. Mainwaring couldn't stop thanking Kenneth for inviting him as the only guest from outside the family.

The bishop himself came to perform the ritual.

Kenneth thought he might drown in the depths of Cat's eyes as they spoke their vows.

When the bishop gave leave for him to kiss his bride, Kenneth felt well and truly married. He savored the applause of his family as he deepened the kiss, his heart and loins rejoicing when Cat suckled his tongue.

After a simple celebratory luncheon, he scooped up his new wife and carried her up the stairs to his bedchamber.

He dismissed the maidservant provided by his mother and set about removing his bride's gown. Her eyes never left his as he bared her body to his gaze. The love he saw burning in those green depths turned the very proper and dignified Duke of Ramsay into a raging inferno of desire.

Hours later, after she'd milked him of his seed more times than he could count, they lay sated in each other's arms. His demure Highland lass had turned out to be an insatiable lover. He was blessed. The long wait to make Cat his was over. Yet, he couldn't shake the vague feeling that something was missing.

"I wish my grandfather could have been here," she whispered into the darkness.

He could have kicked himself. He knew immediately what was missing. Apart from Niven's quiet presence, there'd been nothing remotely Scottish about the entire proceedings. His mind wandered back to Tavish and Piper's wedding in the same drawing room, and the meaningful hand-fasting ceremony Uncle Gregor had performed. Kenneth's bride hadn't uttered a word of complaint, yet he'd deprived her of the right to have family present. "Niven's leaving on the morrow. Why don't we go with him?"

BOTTLES

Alba kept her eyes and ears open each time she visited the distillery. She tried to be discrete when asking questions about the branded bottles the distillery used.

Piper and Tavish often invited her to their home for meals. They were intelligent and friendly, but Payton's occasional presence made conversation awkward. She couldn't seem to control her thoughts when he was around. Piper must deem her a lackwit.

She tried to avoid Payton, but Glengeárr was a small, isolated village and the distillery the only industry.

Despite her best efforts, she learned nothing about the next shipment of bottles.

Then, it dawned on her the answer was perhaps to be found in the ledger to which she had unfettered access. At the first opportunity, she looked back in the records, discouraged to discover the bottles were traditionally ordered only once a year. She slammed the ledger shut when Tavish appeared unexpectedly.

"By the by," he said. "Ye've likely learned we order our bottles from Edinburgh. With the increased business, we're going through our supply at a faster rate than we ever did. I've ordered an extra shipment."

She tried to keep the rising excitement out of her voice. Had he sensed the reason for her interest in the bottles? "And when will they be delivered?"

"Mayhap 'tis a good idea to suggest yon glazier deliver them in future, especially since we're likely to become his biggest customer. For the moment, I send a man to pick them up."

"And when will that be?"

"In about a week," he replied. "Payton has volunteered to go," he added after some hesitation.

Alba's hopes crashed. Payton doubtless thought a journey to Edinburgh would provide them both with a respite from their torment. Tavish had obviously sensed their frustrated attraction to each other and noticed the heated glances. But her plan to escape now seemed impossible. Unless... "Perhaps I could go with him," she suggested, immediately regretting the thoughtless outburst. "Er...it's a chance to see Edinburgh for myself."

Tavish raised an eyebrow, probably thinking she was making matters worse by throwing herself at his brother when, in reality, she was plotting to escape by ship and never see him again. "I'll speak to him," he replied before leaving.

She opened the ledger and stared at the neat rows of figures she'd entered. It was gratifying to know there'd be some record of her brief stay in Glengeárr. She panicked when a tear fell on a recent entry and caused the ink to run.

The suggestion he take Alba with him to Edinburgh had Payton in knots. A few days alone together offered an opportunity to again enjoy the physical pleasures they'd indulged in aboard ship. They wouldn't have to hide their love for each other. They could be themselves.

However, his commitment to Jasmine Foxworthy still haunted him like a specter. He reluctantly acknowledged that his resentment of the situation was quickly turning into hatred for the scatterbrained woman. It was his own fault. "Talk about look before ye leap," he often muttered to himself.

Now, he knew the difference between love and lust. But it was too late.

Weak coward that he was, he couldn't refuse the last chance to bathe in the glow of Alba's love.

"Ye dinna have to take her with ye," Tavish said impatiently.

"Ye want me to say nay," Payton replied, unable to meet his brother's gaze. "But I canna."

Tavish nodded. "I ken how love for a woman can consume a man and I dinna censure ye for it. I still think ye should cancel this ridiculous betrothal, but I willna meddle. I'm just afraid ye'll both end up with broken hearts."

Payton offered his hand. "I'm blessed to have ye as a brother. I'm sorry to have disappointed ye."

Shaking his head, Tavish accepted the handshake and drew Payton into his embrace. "I simply want ye to be happy, and ye ken where yer happiness lies. Ye're a fine man and I'm proud o' ye. I'm lucky to have a brother willing to risk his life to help fulfill my dream."

Payton swallowed the lump in his throat. "Mayhap I should say nay."

"I willna hear o' it. Ye'll take Alba to Edinburgh and hopefully finally realize where yer true duty lies."

～

"Are you sure you want to go on this journey?" Piper asked.

Feigning a last look around the bedchamber to make sure she hadn't forgotten to pack anything, Alba considered her answer.

Long days on the road alone with Payton.

Aye, she wanted that.

A chance to spend a few hours in an inn with the man she would love forever.

Aye. Her body and her heart craved the intimacy.

Deceiving him as to the reason she'd gone along on the errand.

No, the guilt lodged in her throat.

Undertaking a long, cold sea voyage around the northern tip of Scotland.

Her stomach rebelled at the prospect. However, she'd faced hardship before and hoped she had the courage to do it again. Surely a woman who had no trouble outwitting French soldiers could manage to escape Payton?

"*Sí*," she replied to Piper's question. "I am looking forward to seeing Edinburgh."

Piper's frown betrayed her disbelief. "Of course. It's a forlorn hope that you won't both be broken-hearted. Will you try to convince him to abandon Jasmine?"

"No, he must make that decision himself."

Even as she uttered the truth, she knew it was too late for them to find happiness together. If Payton forswore his betrothal to Jasmine, guilt would plague him forever.

COMRADES

Payton and Alba didn't exchange a word of conversation on the first day of the journey to Edinburgh. Her arm linked with his and her head resting on his shoulder said it all. As dusk approached, he made a decision. If they stayed at the usual inn overnight, they'd have to pose as man and wife. "'Tisna rainin' and the skies are clear. Are ye averse to campin' out?" he asked, well aware she'd spent two years living rough in the mountains of Spain.

"You know I'm not," she replied, squeezing his arm more tightly.

Despite the ease between them, he sensed a hint of melancholy in her voice. He too suspected this journey might be the last chance they'd have to be together as lovers.

"If you'd come by yourself, you'd have slept under the stars," she said.

"True," he agreed, pulling off the road into a sheltered copse.

When he lifted her down from the driver's bench, she put her hands over his and leaned into him. Her body against his felt so right, so good. He lacked the will to hold her away, but the horse had to be unhitched and tended to. "I willna be long," he whispered, holding her at arm's length.

Nodding, she walked away. He didn't have to tell her how to prepare for the night. By the time he'd unhitched and fed the horse, she had a fire going and his bed furs spread out over a cushion of heather.

She'd retrieved the sack of provisions from the wagon and had bread and crumbly cheese set out on a fallen log next to a flagon of ale. "Ye are a wonder," he exclaimed.

Her failure to respond was bothersome, but they shared their meal in companionable silence. As darkness fell, he carried her to the bed she'd made and they snuggled together under the furs. Listening to her steady breathing, he gazed up at the stars and knew he would never love another as he loved Alba Castillero. He'd have to make that clear to Jasmine when he saw her. Then it would be up to her to make a decision about the betrothal.

∽

ALBA WAS tired when Payton pulled the wagon into the forecourt of *The White Horse* in the late afternoon. She hadn't slept much the night before, wanting to savor every moment of lying in Payton's arms beneath the twinkling stars. She was apprehensive about entering the inn. No landlord would allow an unmarried man and woman to take rooms, so she and Payton would have to claim they were man and wife. She didn't look upon it as a lie. In her mind, she and Payton were one. The inevitability of sharing a room with him was something she desired but dreaded. It would be their last tryst together.

The innkeeper didn't question their assertion they were married. A young boy showed them up to the room. Payton recognized him. "Cormac, right?" he asked as the lad set about lighting the fire.

"Aye, Sir. Have ye stayed here before?"

"A year or so ago," he replied. "With my brothers and my uncle."

Cormac's eyes brightened. "Aye. I recall ye didna wear drawers neath…er…and ye've married since."

"Aye," Payton replied with a chuckle when Alba and the boy both blushed fiercely.

She perched on the edge of the bed until the lad was satisfied with the progress of the fire and left. Payton came to sit beside her and took hold of her hand. "I'm nay a good liar."

"It isn't a lie," she replied. "You and I belong together."

"I ken it, and I mean to tell Jasmine about ye. Then, 'twill be up to her."

Alba loved him for the sincerity in his eyes, but she forced a smile. His fiancée would never let him go. The general opinion of folk in Glengeárr was that she was more interested in money than in love. "We'll see," she teased. "Meanwhile, *Señor* Payton, *tu eres mio*. You are mine."

"Aye, this night we'll be together, but I recall the landlord here willna allow food to be brought to the rooms, so we're obliged to go down to the dining room before bed."

~

Although Payton longed to get Alba into bed, he savored dining with her. English wasn't her mother tongue, but she understood his jokes and puns better than Jasmine ever had. Her quiet giggling and laughing eyes made him feel like the wittiest man alive. Her table manners were impeccable and he could well imagine the rich, sophisticated lives the Castilleros had lived before the invasion. He'd wager the handsome Pedro Castillero had swept Olivia from Mull off her feet. How else to explain she'd married him and willingly gone to live in faraway Spain —a foreign country very different from her own?

"How do you say in English?" Alba asked with a twinkle in her eyes. "Something about a penny and thinking?"

"A penny for yer thoughts," he replied, realizing he'd been lost in thoughts of making love to her. "I'm thinkin' we should go upstairs."

Arm in arm, they playfully jostled each other on the narrow staircase. He would miss this easy camaraderie— odd to think of a female as a comrade, yet he recognized and was humbled by an inner core of loyalty in her. If he married her, she would be at his side through thick and thin. However, their future was in the hands of a witless lass, thanks to his juvenile preoccupation with big breasts. Now, all he could think of was getting his mouth on Alba's tempting titties—and other, juicier parts of her body.

"*Un centavo por tus pensamientos*," Alba whispered as they stood face to face, holding hands in the silent room.

"My thoughts are worth more than a penny," he teased, leading her to the bed. "Help me get these boots off."

THE WHITE HORSE

Alba had often chafed at her rigid upbringing. Spanish parents were always very strict with their children, especially the daughters. Alba was no exception. She'd been raised to be modest, chaste and obedient. The war had changed things. She'd lived with desperate men and women, and, after all, she was a Spaniard. It was time to let the hot, Spanish blood flow freely in her veins. Scots were passionate people too and she was half Scottish.

She straddled Payton's leg, deliberately wiggling her bottom as she strove to get the boot off his foot. As soon as she succeeded in removing the second boot, he raised her skirts and eased her cheeks apart with his thumbs. Her most private place throbbed with need. Her nipples tingled. "Alba," he growled as he moved quickly to flip her onto her back. He knelt between her legs and put his mouth on the intimate place she'd ached for him to suckle. Summoning her courage, she pulled up her blouse to expose her breasts. His clever fingers played with her nipples and soon she soared with the angels over an Andalusian rainbow and basked in the glow of a golden sunset in the Sierra Morena. In her euphoria, she wasn't certain how he managed to remove her clothes. When she came back to earth, she was lying naked in his arms.

But there should be more. "I want to see you," she whispered, further aroused by the warmth penetrating his woollen trews when she put her hand on him.

"'Tisna a good idea," he rasped. "I might lose what little control I have left."

"*Por favor,* Payton. Let me see."

He stood by the bed, pulled his shirt out of his trews and over his head. She sat up and ran her hands over the fine dusting of dark hair on his broad chest. "*Magnifico,*" she murmured, brushing her thumbs over his nipples.

Inhaling a growled breath, he untied the laces of his trews and shoved them down over his hips. She swallowed hard when his manhood sprang free. "I've glimpsed naked men before in the camps," she admitted, curling her hand around his thick lance. "But I never saw anything as impressive as the king of my heart."

She desperately craved his manhood inside her, but the prospect was more daunting than her mother had led her to believe.

∽

Payton hadn't thought it possible to enjoy heaven and endure hell at the same time. God had been generous with his physical endowments, and the awe in Alba's eyes had his cock in full salute. She was clearly impressed, but afraid as well. "Dinna fash, my little warrior," he whispered. "I willna steal yer maidenhead from yer husband, no matter how badly I want to."

He lost all coherent thought when she kissed the swollen tip of his arousal. Swallowing hard, he hoped words would emerge from his dry mouth. "Ye dinna have to..."

She raised her head, her eyes full of the rapture she'd experienced. "You gave me pleasure this way," she said. "Now, it's my turn to please you. Teach me."

Too weak to resist such a plea, he curled his hand around hers. "Slowly, up and down, like this."

His knees trembled as he entered a new world of physical rapture. "I have to lie down," he growled.

Flat on his back, his heart swelled when she lifted his leg and draped it across her body. Still pumping his cock, she stroked the sensitive skin at the back of his knee and he was lost. He yelled something in Gaelic as his seed erupted from his body and euphoria carried him into ecstasy.

"*Volcán*," she exclaimed.

~

It was past daybreak before Payton stirred in Alba's arms. She'd watched him as he slept, soaking up every feature of his ruggedly handsome face. His male part was resting now, but she would never forget the awesome beauty of his arousal. She was humbled that he'd allowed her to touch the most intimate part of his body and bring him pleasure.

He smiled and sat up when he realized she was watching him. "Ye stay here and rest," he said, licking a nipple. "I'll be gone most of the morning."

She'd anticipated having to beg off the excursion to the glass factory. He'd made it easier. "I'd like to come with you, but I am tired."

As she watched him wash and dress, it was tempting to beg for more physical touching. Her body craved him, but he might sense what she planned.

He kissed her deeply, said goodbye and left.

The tears refused to abate as she washed, dressed and packed her belongings. "*Adiós, mi corazón,*" she whispered as she closed the door to the room and took the stairs down to the front entry. "*Goodbye, my heart.*"

The innkeeper eyed her. "Goin' out, lass?"

"Aye," she replied, striving to sound like her mother. "Can ye direct me to the docks, if ye please?"

He raised a brow. "Aye. Follow the smell o' the sea. Ye canna miss it."

Unwilling to challenge the sarcasm, she nodded and left, a derisive *Foreigners*, echoing in her ears. Attuned to danger by years of guerrilla warfare, she increased her pace when she became aware of malevolent eyes that followed her out of the inn and down the street.

LOST

During the long voyage to Spain, Kenneth had weathered ferocious storms in the Cantabrian Sea, but the gale that tossed Withenshawe's ship in the North Sea was worse. He was normally a good sailor, even in rough seas, but he, Niven and Cat all succumbed to *mal-de-mer*.

When the wind tore the schooner's mainsail, he feared he might not get to enjoy the euphoria of his newly married status for very long. He tried not to show his nervousness, but doubted the perceptive Cat was fooled. She had a canny knack of knowing exactly how he was feeling and what he was thinking. They were ideally matched in that regard. He sensed her every emotion.

It therefore came as a relief when the captain informed them he'd have to head for Edinburgh for repairs. "We'll not make it to Dundee in this weather," he said.

"I've never been to Edinburgh," Cat murmured bravely.

"I'm sure Withenshawe will provide us with transport to Glengeárr," he replied, taking her into his arms. "But we can stay in the city a day or two."

"My brothers and I lodged at *The White Horse* on our way to London," Niven told them. "It's an old place, but the food's decent."

"*The White Horse* it is, then," Kenneth declared, praying the stricken ship would make it to the Edinburgh docks in Leith.

He breathed more easily when the vessel entered the Firth. The winds eased and the waves no longer threatened to overwhelm the schooner. Crewmen were able to lower the torn sail.

Withenshawe maintained only one dock and a skeleton staff in Edinburgh. It therefore took a few hours for the travelers to disembark and find transport to *The White Horse*.

~

THERE WERE signs of autumn in the air by the time Alba reached the docks at Leith in mid-afternoon. She'd lost her bearings several times and had to ask for directions which didn't always turn out to be correct. She'd walked much further than anticipated. Born and bred in Spain, she had no tolerance for the chilly wind from which Piper's meager shawl did little to protect her. The cold in her bones was aggravated by the certainty someone was following her.

She dodged in and out of shadowy doorways but, when she risked a furtive glance over her shoulder, he was still dogging her steps.

She didn't know if she could trust the shifty-looking, grubby men working on the docks, but she had to find the ship was that would take her to Mull. She finally approached an elderly, bearded fellow perched on a wooden piling, skinny legs dangling. "Kind sir, can ye point me in the direction o' the ship bound for Mull?" she asked.

He took the pipe out of his mouth, spat on the ground and muttered, "Nay."

"Ye dinna ken where 'tis?"

"Ye'er nay from these parts, I'm guessin'," he replied.

So much for the effectiveness of her brogue.

"No, but I have to get to my aunty's house in Mull."

"Then ye'll have to wait 'til spring. They dinna sail the northern route at this time o' year. Sea's already rough. See them whitecaps?" He pointed to a nearby ship. "Yon schooner got its sail torn by the wind comin' fra' London."

Panic tightened the knot in Alba's stomach. She didn't have the energy nor the will to walk back to the inn, and her malevolent shadow still lurked nearby.

"I'm a stranger to this area," she confessed, hoping she could trust him. "Do you know of an inn hereabouts?"

"Aye, sev'ral, but they're nay the kind o' place a lass like ye wants to stay, lest ye're looking to make extra coin."

Bile rose up Alba's throat. She had a dagger lashed to

her thigh but didn't relish the prospect of using it to fend off men in a brothel. She'd be one against many. "I suppose I'll make my way back to *The White Horse*."

"Nay," he replied. "Too far. Stay at my place, if ye like. Set out on the morrow."

She dithered. "Do you live close by?"

"I've a wee shanty not far from the docks." He relieved her of the valise clutched to her chest. "Come on."

She had no choice but to follow him as he shuffled off. On the morrow, she'd have to figure out another way to get to Mull—if she survived the night.

～

LOADING the crates of bottles took longer than Payton had anticipated. He was further delayed when the owner of the glass company wanted to discuss future orders. When the jovial fellow insisted on sharing a dram or two of his own stock of *Uachdaran*, Payton could hardly say nay.

As a result, he lost his way twice during the return journey to the inn. He finally drove into the stables behind the inn as previously arranged with the innkeeper. Securing the wagon and its precious load took time during which he chunnered about the steep price exacted for the security. He was grateful when an ostler offered to take care of the horse. Bothered by a vague sense of impending doom, he was so impatient to see Alba again, he almost didn't notice a group of people arguing with the innkeeper until one indignant voice rose above the others.

"Now, look here, my good man."

Payton stopped his headlong rush to the stairs. He knew that voice. "Kenneth?"

Three heads turned toward him.

"Niven? Cat?"

His younger brother was hugging him before he had a chance to say anything more. Exchanging hugs and handshakes, they all started talking at once. Payton gradually understood the circumstances that had brought the others to Edinburgh and he explained his errand to fetch the bottles. He congratulated Kenneth and Cat on their marriage. The sour-faced innkeeper looked on.

Suddenly, a frown replaced Niven's grin. "We came to tell ye something important," he said. "I wanted ye to hear it from me."

Payton couldn't imagine what dire tidings had brought his wee brother to Scotland, but he braced himself for the bad news he'd sensed was coming. "Tell me."

SHANTY

"Jasmine is married to someone else?" Payton asked, scarcely able to believe what Niven had told him.

"The Earl o' Waterdown," his brother replied. "Daisy and I attended the ceremony so I can vouch 'tis true."

"Weel, bugger me," Payton exclaimed, torn between anger at the fickle woman's treachery and elation that he was at last free. "I aimed to tell her about Alba and let her decide about our future."

"She's obviously made her decision," Kenneth replied.

"I must tell Alba the good news," he declared, heading for the stairs.

"She's here?" Niven asked.

"Aye, she's..."

"Nay," the innkeeper interjected. "The foreign lass went out and hasna come back."

Payton's hackles rose. "I dinna care for the way ye

spat out the word *foreign*," he hissed, standing nose to nose with the landlord. "Where did she go?"

"How would I ken?" came the shrugged response.

Payton's mind whirled. He couldn't organize his thoughts. Had Alba really left him? Could he blame her?

"How long ago did she leave?" Kenneth asked.

"A few hours. Now, do ye folk want a room or nay?"

Payton vaguely heard Kenneth arrange for a room for Cat, then his cousin and his brother were dragging him outside. "We'll find her," Niven assured him.

"We dinna ken where she's gone," Payton retorted. "'Tis my fault. I was too weak to commit myself to her. I kept holdin' Jasmine o'er her head."

"You were trying to do the honorable thing," Kenneth argued. "Now, we must think where she might have gone."

Payton felt a tug on his jacket sleeve, surprised when he looked down to see young Cormac at his side.

"Yer lady asked directions to the docks," the lad whispered. "Da's just bein' ornery."

Fear gripped Payton's vitals. Alba was alone in a strange city, apparently searching for the docks—probably the worst place she could be headed for.

"*Crivvens*," Niven exclaimed. "I wouldna want to be wanderin' around those docks. Too many seedy characters hangin' about. We just came from there."

"Let's not panic," Kenneth said. "Do you suppose she's trying to return to Spain?"

Payton closed his eyes and forced himself to think. "Nay. I'd wager she's plannin' to sail to Mull."

"In this weather?" Kenneth exclaimed. "Our schooner barely made it as far as Edinburgh."

"I'd be surprised if any ship e'en sails the northern route at this time o' year," Niven said.

Payton felt as though every drop of blood had drained from his body into his feet. They were lead weights incapable of movement. But he had to move, had to find the woman he loved before he lost her forever. She was courageous and canny enough to navigate the dangers of war in Spain, but she'd be easy pickings for any ne'er-do-well in the city's dockland slums.

"We'll need transport," Kenneth declared, heading into the inn.

"Round back," Payton replied. "I've a wagon. 'Twill be quicker than waiting for yon disagreeable landlord to find us a carriage."

"I'll help ye wi' the nag," Cormac said.

~

ALBA HADN'T UNDERSTOOD the word *shanty* and still didn't when the old man led her to a tiny structure that looked like it might collapse at any moment. There was still enough daylight to make out that the dwelling was made from scavenged materials—driftwood and other things she couldn't identify. It was one of several similar but slightly different structures heaped together a little way beyond the docks.

"Doesna look like much," he said, moving aside a wooden panel that apparently served as the door. "But ye'll be out o' the weather."

As a partisan, Alba had slept in worse conditions. She had no choice but to trust the old fellow. "My name is Alba," she said. "I'm from Spain."

"Spanish, eh? Better off in Leith. Terrible business with Napoleon. Ye can call me Donald."

"My mother was from Mull," she explained as he ushered her into the dark interior.

"I see," he replied.

Though it was still daylight, she couldn't make out anything until he lit a candle stub. Donald lived in an empty box. Given what she'd been told about Scottish winters, it was a wonder he didn't freeze to death. She'd seen poverty in Spain, but at least poor people there didn't have to cope with cold weather.

She was hesitant to tell him about the man who'd been following her. He might view it as a threat to himself. "It's good of you to shelter me," she said, eyeing the still-open doorway.

"Nobody'll bother ye," he replied, shoving the door back in place. "Sit ye doon."

There was nothing to sit on, so she joined him and sat cross-legged on the dirt floor.

"Hungry?" he asked.

"Ravenous," she replied, regretting it when his toothless smile disappeared.

"Sorry I've naught but this stale loaf," he said, removing a heel of bread from inside his coat.

She'd gone without food many a time and he'd likely eaten nothing else all day. "You enjoy it," she said. "I'm all right."

"Nay," he replied, breaking off a chunk and handing it to her.

Grateful for the gathering darkness, she chewed the rock-hard bread until it eventually became soft enough to swallow.

The meager candle guttered out. Before long, the sound of his snoring convinced her she may as well lie down and try to sleep. Tears flowed when she thought of how angry Payton must have been to discover her gone. She'd handled things badly and now found herself in an impossible situation. She could only pray the man she loved would forgive the betrayal. But how would he find her in this hovel? Would he even come looking?

RESCUE

Payton was tempted to chuck every crate of empty bottles into the street in order to lighten the wagon's load. Tavish would never forgive him. He could make up some plausible tale, but Niven was with him and his younger brother was a terrible liar.

After an eternity which saw them stop for directions several times in Edinburgh's warren of unbelievably tall tenements, they arrived in dockland. Darkness had fallen and the area was mostly deserted, except for a few shadowy figures lurking here and there. Cats screeched. Waves lapped at the wooden pilings. The reek of fish guts was overpowering.

Pointing out the schooner that had suffered the torn sail, Kenneth suggested they separate to begin searching.

"I think we should stick together," Niven countered. "This isna a place for a man to be alone."

Payton knew his brother hadn't meant to make him feel worse, but he did. Alba was clever and had probably armed herself, but a woman was no match for gangs of dockland thugs intent on mischief. "I agree," he replied. "We'll stay together."

"I shouldn't think she's on the docks themselves," Kenneth said. "Unless she stowed away on a vessel, or the ship to the Isles has sailed."

"Doubtful," Payton replied, narrowing his eyes to peer into the darkness. "Let's search over by yon shanties."

∼

ALBA WAS USED to sleeping with one eye open. In Spain, being alert to various noises had often meant the difference between life and death. Considering the shanty was close to docks that were busy during the day, the silence was eerie. She heard only Donald's soft snoring and the wind whistling across the water.

Yet, there was movement outside—and too close for comfort.

She scrambled to her knees and listened.

A footfall.

The stink of an unwashed body.

Heavy breathing.

The scrape of wood on wood.

Someone was trying to get into the shanty.

When Donald stopped snoring, she'd wager he'd heard the noises too. A man who slept alone in such a place would have to keep his wits about him. Not that he had anything to steal. Reality struck her like a blow to the belly. The intruder had come for her, not for any possessions Donald might have.

She unsheathed her dagger, crouched and waited.

When she heard the sickening sound of flesh striking flesh and Donald's groans of pain, she sprang up and launched herself onto the intruder. "*Leave him alone,*" she shrieked. "*Déjalo en paz.*"

~

Payton swiveled his head to the shanty where he thought the shouting had come from. There could only be one person screaming in Spanish. "Over here," he yelled to Kenneth and Niven, thrusting aside what might once have been a makeshift door.

He peered into the dark shanty, his heart in his throat. An old man lay at his feet, groaning loudly. Was he an attacker, or...

A shaky voice broke the silence. "Don't come any closer, or I'll slit his throat."

"Alba?" he rasped as he ventured further into the hovel.

When his eyes grew accustomed to the darkness, he nigh on laughed out loud. Alba had an arm clamped under the quivering chin of a burly fellow. The point of her dagger was pressed to the thug's throat.

Payton held up a restraining hand when Kenneth and Niven rushed in behind him. "I think my warrior has things under control," he said.

"Payton?" she murmured. "Is that you?"

"Aye, *mi amor.* 'Tis me."

He was bursting to tell her about Jasmine, but she stared into nothingness, seemingly in a trance. He gently eased the weapon from her hand and uncoiled her arm from the brute's neck. Kenneth and Niven took hold and wrestled the sobbing wretch out of the shanty.

"Donald's hurt," she said softly. "We must take care of him. He was kind enough to offer me shelter."

The old man staggered to his feet. "I'm all reet," he croaked. "Teck care o' the lass. She saved us both."

Alba remained silent. Recognizing she was in shock after her ordeal, Payton picked her up and carried her out of the shanty.

~

Alba didn't know where she was when she woke. A strange clinking noise rang in her ears. She was in some kind of moving conveyance and couldn't keep her eyes open. She had never felt so tired in her life. "Where am I," she murmured.

"In a wagon full of glass bottles," a voice replied. "We'll soon be at the inn."

It couldn't be Payton who held her in his arms. She'd left him.

"Aye, ye're safe wi' me. Kenneth is drivin'."

"Kenneth is here?"

"Aye. And Niven."

"Who?"

"My brother."

"I left Payton. Is this Mull?"

"Nay. Rest now."

The fog was too tempting to resist so she allowed it to carry her into sleep.

Lording it over the sulking landlord, Kenneth provided a welcome distraction as Payton carried Alba up the stairs to their room at the inn. Cat appeared at the doorway of another room further down the hallway and smiled when she saw he'd found Alba. "She's had a scare, but she's fine," he said softly. "I'll introduce ye on the morrow. Kenneth's downstairs."

She nodded and closed her door.

Payton carefully lay his precious burden on the bed, curled up beside her and dragged the covers over them both. Cocooned in the blankets with Alba in his arms, he thanked God for the promise of years of happiness with the woman he loved. He'd tell her the good news when she was feeling more herself.

EACH TO HIS OWN

"Why did you not tell me last night?" Alba exclaimed.

"Weel," Payton began.

"Did you not think I'd want to know that the man I love can be mine after all?"

"I..."

"You let me spend the night worrying about how I was going to escape again?"

"Ye slept..."

"That isn't the point!"

"Dinna be angry wi' me," he pleaded after touching his finger to her lips. "I simply wanted ye to be wide awake and away from that hovel when I told ye about Jasmine."

"How dare that selfish woman jilt you!"

The rumble of Payton's hearty laughter broke the spell Alba had cast on herself. She too heard how ridiculous her complaints sounded. Sharing his laughter, she melted into his arms. "*Te adoro, rey de mi corazón.*"

"Weel, my name *is* King," he chuckled. "So, I suppose 'tis only right I be *king o' yer heart.*"

Alba's joy knew no bounds. "You understood what I said in Spanish."

"I'm learnin', *mo chridhe,*" he replied with a smile.

"'Tis Gaelic for heart," he explained in answer to her puzzled frown. "I'll learn to speak Spanish, and you can learn Gaelic."

"I'll try," she agreed. "My mother didn't speak Gaelic."

"I'll teach ye," he offered.

"I hope you'll teach me lots of things," she murmured shyly. "My mother told me a little bit about marriage, but..."

"'Twill be my honor and my pleasure," he promised. "Does this mean ye'll be my bride?"

"*Sí*, a thousand times, aye," she replied, taking his beloved face in her hands. "Let's hurry back to your kingdom in Glengeárr," she whispered, knowing he would appreciate the play on words.

"*Crivvens*, what a prize I have in ye," he exclaimed with a broad grin. "I'm plannin' to marry ye as soon as possible. I've wasted too much time already. Kenneth is in a hurry to get back. However, there's something we must do first."

∾

Watching Alba wash and dress, Payton tucked away her clever use of his family name. It gave him an idea—

something he might suggest to Tavish and Niven once they got home.

"I'm going back to the glassworks," he told her once he too was dressed.

"*Por qué?*" she asked.

"The owner is a charitable man. I'll ask Jameson to give yer Donald a chance."

"Thank you," she replied. "He took a risk. I think he knew the man was following me, but he tried to protect me—and got beaten for his kindness."

"I make no promises, mind," he added. "'Twill be for Jameson to decide."

"And I promise not to run away again," she said coyly.

"Kenneth, Niven and Cat will make sure of it," he warned with a wink.

"I'd like the chance to get to know them, but I'd prefer to come with you. I need to thank Donald and make sure he is all right."

"Ye saved his life," he retorted.

"But I put it at risk."

Payton accepted that he wasn't going to win the argument. They tiptoed past Kenneth and Cat's room. "No sign o' life yet," he quipped.

That brought to mind the question of where his younger brother had spent the night. The answer came when they bumped into Niven on his way out of the stables. "Ye've straw in yer hair," Payton exclaimed. "Surely ye didna sleep wi' the nags."

"Aye. Yon landlord claimed to have no rooms left."

Payton felt badly. He hadn't given a thought to his brother's accommodations.

"Dinna fash," Niven said. "Ye'd enough to worry about and I'm glad to finally meet Alba."

Payton experienced a ridiculous pang of jealousy when his brother and Alba shared a warm embrace.

"And I am very happy to meet you," Alba said. "Payton has talked about you a lot and I can see the family likeness."

"People say Tavish, Niven and I look alike," Payton said. "Funny thing is, we canna see it."

"Aye. Where are ye off to?" Niven asked.

Payton invited him to come along on the errand, but Niven declined. "I want to find out if they've made progress repairin' the torn sail."

"Seems optimistic to me," Alba whispered once she'd settled on the driver's bench.

"Me too," Payton agreed as he watched his brother saunter out of the stable.

∽

IN THE FULL light of day, Donald's shanty looked even more dilapidated. Alba scanned the neighboring docks and the other makeshift dwellings. "It's truly a miracle I survived," she admitted. "It was foolish of me to come here."

"Ye weren't thinkin' straight," Payton allowed, nodding to Donald when the old man shuffled out of his box.

The muck on his face and the overgrown beard hid

any bruising he might have suffered from the attack. The scowl fled and he straightened his shoulders when he espied Alba. "'Tis good to see ye recovered, Lass. Will this bonny laddie be takin' ye to Mull?"

"No, Donald. There was a misunderstanding. Me and this *bonny laddie* will be getting married in Glengeárr."

"Why do ye want to go to such a remote place?" he asked, scratching his head.

"My brothers and I operate a whisky distillery there," Payton explained. "'Tis the reason for all the bottles."

Donald licked his lips. "'Tis a long while since I had a wee dram o' whisky."

"Ours is called *Uachdaran*."

Donald closed his eyes and sighed. "The finest single malt I ever did taste."

"Actually," Payton interjected. "We came to thank ye fer offerin' shelter. We had an idea to ask Jameson at the glassworks if he has a job fer ye."

"Nay need fer thanks. 'Twas the lassie saved us both. I suppose ye learned to fight bullies in Spain."

"Aye," she replied with a smile. "French bullies."

"Cursed Napoleon," he exclaimed.

Payton gritted his teeth. Alba sensed his impatience.

"We should be getting back to the inn to devise a plan for returning to the Highlands," he said close to her ear. "Five people traveling in a wagon full of bottles will result in a lot of discomfort." He turned to Donald. "So, do ye want a job or nay?"

The elderly fellow shook his head. "Good man yon Jameson Buchanan, but I'm too old for liftin' stuff. I earn a little here and there on the docks. 'Tis enough for me."

"Are you certain?" Alba asked. "I don't like to leave you here."

He shifted his puzzled gaze to the shanty. "Aye, weel, 'tis home, ye ken."

Payton took her arm and led her to the wagon. "Goodbye, then, Donald."

"*Soraidh*," he replied.

"What does that mean?" Alba asked as she climbed aboard.

"Farewell."

"*Soraidh*," she told the old man.

"Each to his own," Payton said as they drove away.

"There is kindness everywhere if you look for it," she replied.

∼

PAYTON INTENDED to stop by *The White Horse* for a short while to consult with Kenneth and Niven. However, Cormac approached him in the yard behind the inn and handed over a letter as soon as he climbed down from the bench. "Yon duke gave it to me 'cos he didna trust my Da to pass it on."

Payton flipped him a coin and opened the envelope as the lad strolled away whistling.

"Why has Kenneth written to you?" Alba asked.

Payton scanned the short missive. "They had to leave. The sail was repaired more quickly than anticipated and the captain insisted on leaving with the tide. My cousin assumes he'll arrive in Glengeárr before us and will have everything arranged for our wedding when we get there."

"Niven has gone too?" she asked.

"Aye. 'Twill just be ye and me on the road to the Highlands."

"I can't think of anyone I'd rather travel with," she quipped with a grin.

REUNION

"I'm nervous about returning to Glengeárr," Cat confessed as the schooner bumped against the dock at Dundee.

Her husband took her into his embrace and turned to shelter her from the chilly wind. "You're afraid local people will think you've reached above your station," he replied.

"Which is true."

"Some might think that, but those who matter won't. Tavish, Piper and anyone who truly knows you will be very pleased to see us together. And Uncle Gregor will be delighted to learn we've come all this way so he can recite the magic words to bless our marriage."

Niven joined them at the rail. "I'll have a few choice words to say to anyone who criticizes ye," he said.

"As will I," Kenneth confirmed.

"Folk will be excited by the prospect of two of Glengeárr's young folk gettin' hitched," Niven added. "They've ne'er seen the like."

"That just leaves ye, Niven," Cat said.

"Nay," he replied. "I'll ne'er wed."

"We'll see," she said. "Things dinna always turn out the way ye expect."

Kenneth wiggled his eyebrows. "Too true. Anyway, I have a little surprise in my baggage that will keep tongues wagging about something other than weddings."

"Like what?" Niven asked.

"Wait and see," Kenneth replied.

Cat was puzzled. She and her husband shared everything but, apparently, he'd been keeping a secret.

~

A DAY and a half after finally docking in Dundee, Kenneth, Cat and Niven arrived in Glengeárr shortly after midday. They'd traveled in comfort thanks to the provision of a carriage by Withenshawe's people who apologized profusely for the inconvenience of the unscheduled stop in Edinburgh. Kenneth deemed it preferable not to mention the torn sail had proven to be a godsend. Who could say what might have become of Alba had he and Niven not been in Edinburgh to assist Payton in his search?

Kenneth was proud of the humble and gracious way his duchess reacted to the deferential treatment. "You're a natural," he told her.

He directed the driver to Lockie House, thinking to provide his wife with an opportunity to refresh herself in his mother's refurbished ancestral home. Niven decided to walk to the distillery to reunite with his brother.

"I'll hire a maidservant once we get settled," Kenneth suggested to Cat when she set about unpacking their valises.

"Nay," she replied with a saucy grin. "I can manage. I have a husband keen to help dress and undress me should the need arise."

He suspected she didn't want to employ a local girl who might resent serving a commoner turned duchess, but he was more than happy to take on the role of lady's maid. "I think I have the hang of the tapes and laces," he quipped. "And I'm a whiz at corsets..."

The heated kiss they shared might have led to bedsport had a loud knock not resounded at the front door. They set their clothing to rights and arrived downstairs in time for his mother's butler to announce Tavish and Piper King and their son, Munro.

"Yes, thank you, MacBeth," Kenneth said, embarrassed by the unnecessary formality.

"Such a fuss," Uncle Gregor declared as he appeared at the top of the stairs and began the slow descent.

MacBeth had informed them Gregor was asleep when they arrived, so they hadn't wanted to wake him. Kenneth noticed he relied heavily on his cane.

Piper passed Munro to her husband and rushed to hug Cat. "I'm so glad to see you, my friend, or should I say Your Grace?"

"I'll clobber ye if ye call me that," Cat replied, taking Munro from Tavish. "'Tis good to be home. This wee one is going to be a bonny lad."

"Your grandad will be overjoyed to see you," Piper said.

Kenneth wasn't surprised to see his wife's chin quiver, but his loins were preoccupied with the sight of her holding Tavish's son. The thought of her round with his child made him sweat.

He shook Gregor's hand when his uncle made it to the bottom of the stairs then he and Tavish exchanged a hearty embrace. "We've news to impart," Kenneth told everyone. "First off, our schooner suffered a torn sail and docked in Edinburgh on the way to Dundee. We were lucky to bump into Payton there. We informed him Jasmine has married someone else."

"Saints be praised," Tavish exclaimed.

Munro gurgled his approval.

"I sensed Jasmine wasn't to be trusted," Piper echoed. "So, Payton and Alba..."

"Aye," Cat replied. "There was a hitch that had to be overcome. They're on their way from Edinburgh and they'll tell ye about it but, first, I must share with ye the reason we came to Scotland."

"Aye, Uncle Gregor," Kenneth explained, "we want ye to say the ancient words to bless our marriage."

His uncle's eyes filled with tears. "'Twill be my honor."

"You can perform the ceremony for Payton and Alba at the same time," Piper suggested.

Excited chatter ensued. Cat asked MacBeth to bring tea to the drawing room. Tavish produced a bottle of *Uachdaran*.

While his loved ones sipped tea and whisky, Kenneth

watched his wife playing with Munro on the carpet. His heart was full. Cat was going to be a wonderful mother to his children. The upcoming hand-fasting ceremonies promised joy and augured well for the future. The surprise he'd brought from London would be the icing on the cake.

PREPARATIONS FOR THE BIG DAY

En route to Glengeárr, Payton and Alba spent the night cuddled together neath the stars. "I feel reborn," Payton whispered, pulling her closer when the wind picked up.

"*Yo también*," she agreed, snuggling into his warmth. "My mother would be delighted if she knew I am to wed a Scot."

"Scotland was yer destiny."

"You are my destiny, Payton," she replied. "I realize now my father sensed it."

He grieved for her pain. "Ye'll see him again. We'll go back to Spain when the war is over."

"That might not be for a long time," she sighed.

"Ye could be right," he replied reluctantly. "There was talk at the glassworks of a French victory in the north. They held on to Burgos when Wellington was forced to retreat into Portugal to avoid having his troops encircled."

"Napoleon will not give up easily."

He searched for something to say that would ease her melancholy. "I suspect ye're right, but mayhap by then our bairns will be old enough to travel with us when we sail to Spain."

It was a while before she asked, "How many *niños* would you like?"

"Three boys, for sure."

"Like you and your brothers."

"Aye. And three wee lasses who will be as bonny as their mother."

"I agree," she chuckled. "I always longed for a sister. You'll be a good father."

His heart swelled with the certainty she was right. He was determined to do a better job than his own parents.

They talked for a while, pointing out the constellations above them, until clouds obscured the stars and it began to rain. Laughing, they gathered up the furs, ran for the wagon and sheltered under the tarpaulin, content to cuddle in each other's arms until daybreak. Now he was certain Alba would truly be his, the desperate urge to possess her wasn't as keen—with a supreme effort he could wait until they married.

~

ALBA PUT her hand on Payton's arm when Glengeárr came into view late the next afternoon. "I beg you not to tell them I ran away from you," she pleaded.

"'Tisna something I'll be anxious to boast about," Payton replied with a wry smile. "But Kenneth, Cat and

Niven may already have told folk about our misadventure."

"Please ask them not to say anything if they haven't already."

"Dinna fash. The gossip is more likely to be about Jasmine and nay ye. If anyone is at fault, 'tis me. I was too weak to make a clean break with Miss Foxworthy."

"No. Your determination to do the honorable thing was a sign of strength, not weakness."

"Weel, 'tis water under the bridge, as they say. People here will be happy for us," he said as they came to a halt in front of the distillery.

Tavish hurried out to meet them. "My thanks to the pair o' ye," he exclaimed. "Niven told me he'd run into ye in Edinburgh."

"Aye," Payton confirmed warily as he helped Alba alight. "'Twas a coincidence."

Workmen came out to assist with unloading the new bottles. Kenneth followed and took Alba aside. "We didn't say anything about what transpired in Edinburgh."

"I'm grateful," she replied. "I realize now how foolish I was."

"But you weren't to know at the time that Jasmine had married another man."

Smiling his reassurance, he left her to help the workers.

Niven appeared and winked at her before he too set about hefting crates of bottles.

Alba breathed more easily. Her impetuous folly had not become general knowledge.

~

For two days, Piper, Cat and Alba were completely preoccupied with preparations for the hand-fasting to be conducted by Uncle Gregor. The old man himself could talk of naught else.

Mindful of the fact Alba was of the Catholic faith, Payton made arrangements with the priest at Craigdarroch Castle to come to Glengeárr to bless their union. He was glad of it. Like most Highlanders, generations of the King family had remained true to the Catholic faith, though their attendance at Mass had lapsed, even before the advent of Walter and Moira's sneering disregard for organized religion. They were too busy fighting with each other to tend to Christian duties.

Payton felt a sense of correctness about securing the Church's blessing, especially after he gave his bride the parcel her father had entrusted to him. It contained a large piece of black lace which reduced her to tears as soon as she saw it. "It was my mother's *mantilla*," she gasped. "Now, I'll look like a true bride and I'll feel her presence when we wed. My father must have known we would marry. He would never have surrendered this to you otherwise."

Much to Tavish's annoyance, Payton begged off assisting with time-consuming tasks in the distillery, confident his older brother would understand when he learned what Payton was up to at the local sign painter's premises.

He confided in Kenneth that he had a special surprise planned for the morning of the wedding.

"Good to know," his cousin replied. "I've a presentation of my own to carry out. I'll wait until then."

Payton's reaction was mixed. "I hope ye willna upstage me."

"I might," Kenneth replied with a chuckle.

~

"'Twas the only drawback to marrying a duke," Cat explained, as she plied her needle.

"What was that?" Piper asked, her question muffled by the straight pins in her mouth.

"I wasna allowed to sew my own gown."

"*Bueno*," Alba said. "My sewing skills are rather rusty, so I appreciate your help making my dress."

"I dinna suppose there was much call for a seamstress on the battlefields of Spain," Cat quipped.

"*Verdad*," Alba confirmed. "Though I was called upon to sew up a few nasty wounds."

Cat felt chastened after that remark, so silence reigned for a while in the drawing room of Lockie House.

"We dinna have much available here to fashion a really spectacular dress," Piper lamented.

"I will feel marvelous in what you are creating," Alba replied. "I lost most of my good clothes when the French destroyed our *bodega*. A black dress is traditional for Spanish brides. It signifies commitment and devotion until death."

"We've tried to make something along the lines of the traditional Spanish dress as ye've described it," Cat said. "Let's try it on and see what we think."

THE BIG REVEAL

Tavish paced his living room while he waited for his wife to return from dressing the bride upstairs. "Payton is up to something," he told her when she appeared at the foot of the stairs.

"What makes you think that?" Piper replied.

"'Tisna like him to shirk jobs in the distillery. However, he's getting married today, so I'm willin' to make allowances." He took Piper into his arms. "I remember how besotted I was the day we married. I couldna think straight."

"When Payton sets his eyes on Alba's gown, he'll have the same trouble," she teased.

"I'm nay sure why my brother insists on starting the ceremony in front o' the distillery," Tavish groused. "He and Niven have been gone since dawn. And this mornin', I'm nay allowed to go near my own distillery? I ask ye."

Cat joined them as she came downstairs. "I overheard and I must say Kenneth has been acting just as strangely. He's been keeping some secret since he called on the Regent in London."

"Exciting," Piper exclaimed.

Tavish tamped down his irritation. He was letting off steam in front of two beautiful women elegantly dressed for a wedding. Not only that, Cat was probably nervously excited about the hand-fasting Gregor was to perform for her and Kenneth. "Forgive me," he begged, taking his wife's hand. "This day isna about me."

Piper's indulgent smile had the usual effect on his loins, but Kenneth's abrupt arrival banished any thoughts of whisking her upstairs for a quick tryst.

"Right," his breathless cousin exclaimed. "Piper, ye can fetch the bride and we'll escort her to the…er… distillery. Tavish, ye can take Cat there now, then stand with yer brother, the groom."

"Suddenly, ye're a Scot," Tavish retorted. "And a bossy one at that."

His wife's glare told him he'd gone too far. He composed himself and offered his arm to Cat. "Come along, Yer Grace," he said. "Let's see what mischief they've been up to."

~

KENNETH STOOD at the bottom of Tavish's stairs waiting for the bride. It occurred to him that his Scottish blood did tend to assert itself when he was excited. But this was a day for excitement. Momentous events were about to take place. Tavish was irritated now but Kenneth would warrant he'd be thrilled by the surprises he and

Payton had in store for him. And if a duke couldn't be bossy on such a day, well...

He forgot his next thought when a smiling Alba appeared at the head of the stairs. A thousand memories of Spain crowded into his brain—a ruined *bodega*, the taste of fine sherry, scorched vines struggling to be reborn, men dragging a cannon over impossible terrain, stunning sunsets, the unrelenting heat, the determination to take back their country etched on every partisan's face.

This diminutive woman had saved his and Payton's lives and shown more courage than most men of his acquaintance. His cousin was a lucky man. Kenneth uttered a silent prayer of thanks that Jasmine Foxworthy had been too scatterbrained to realize what a prize she had in Payton King. Alba, on the other hand, would fit right into this little corner of Scotland.

"*Señorita* Castillero," he said, offering his arm. "'Twill be my honor and my pleasure to give ye away to my cousin."

"I never imagined I would walk to my wedding on the arm of a *duque*," she replied. "It's you who honor me, *Estimado Amigo*."

"I don't suppose you thought you'd be getting married in a distillery, either," Piper remarked as the trio left the house.

∽

ALBA DIDN'T WISH to contradict Piper, but her dream had always been to marry in a distillery—at least in the *bodega* where she'd been born. Napoleon had killed that dream, but this place, this remote corner of Scotland, was even better. This was where she would live her life with a man she loved, a man who distilled whisky. It might not be sherry but it was close enough.

She'd expected to be escorted into the distillery itself and was puzzled to see a large crowd standing outside. The excited chatter ceased when they caught sight of her. The crowd parted and Kenneth escorted her to stand beside Payton. Dragging her gaze away from the laughing eyes of her handsome groom, she looked up at the wall.

Two black cloths had been draped over something affixed to the ancient stones.

"*Qué es esto?*" she asked. "What...?"

Payton squeezed her hand. "Patience," he whispered close to her ear.

She grew even more confused when he patted her hand then left her side to take up a stance in front of the gathering. The rugged Scot standing with powerful legs braced and looking magnificent in his Highland regalia was soon to be her husband. Her nipples tightened and her intimate woman's place throbbed with anticipation.

"Friends and relatives," he began, his deep voice washing over her. "Ye ken 'tis customary for a groom to give his bride a wedding gift." He arched an eyebrow. "I mean apart from the obvious."

Grunts of agreement and tittered laughter greeted his bawdy jest. Alba blushed but couldn't think what gift would be concealed behind the black drapes.

"My gift is a wee bit unusual. 'Tis for my bride, but also for my brothers. Step forward, Tavish and Niven."

Alba held her breath when the two frowning men joined him and Payton took hold of a corner of one drape.

Applause followed a collective gasp of approval when he snatched away the fabric to reveal what was fixed to the wall.

Alba read the bold black letters painted on the large wooden sign.

KINGDOM DISTILLERY
Home of Uachdaran Single Malt Whisky

She understood Tavish and Niven's proud delight as they shook Payton's hand. She would never reveal it was she who'd first spoken of the Kings' Kingdom. Payton had obviously not forgotten her father's ruined sign.

However, it was the detail painted in red beneath that made her heart swell. Scarcely able to breath, she read Payton's precious gift to her.

Agents for Bodegas Castillero
Purveyors of Fine Spanish Sherry

The defiant little flag of her homeland in one corner reduced her to tears.

"*Gracias,*" she croaked when Payton took her in his arms.

"*De nada, mi amor,*" he replied.

She'd thought the surprises over but a hush fell when

Kenneth stood before the gathering and cleared his throat.

"Of course," she said. "The other drapery."

"Aye. My cousin's a wee bit miffed that I insisted my sign be revealed first."

She squealed her delight when Kenneth dragged away the covering. Affixed to the wall was a magnificent embossed crimson shield edged in gold. A coat of arms sat front and center. Above it gold letters declared

∼

WHISKY DISTILLERS

"The most important words are below the coat of arms," Payton explained. "By Royal Appointment."

"His Majesty the Prince Regent sends his regards to Glengeárr," Kenneth shouted. "And wishes He could be present on this memorable day."

Loud cheering resounded as Payton and Kenneth escorted their brides into the distillery.

RITUALS

Tavish gazed around his distillery, scarcely able to believe this was the place where he spent most of his life. Many hands had been busy festooning the space in front of the kettles with bunting. Candles burned brightly. His place of work had been transformed into a cathedral. It was fitting. He'd always considered the distilling of whisky a sacred task, a magical transformation of barley into *Uisge Beatha*, the Water of Life.

He wasn't the only one gawking with amazed awe. But three people looked hot and bothered as they strode toward him—Payton, Uncle Gregor and the priest from Craigdarroch.

"What's amiss?" Tavish asked, worried when he espied Kenneth chewing his lip. He wouldn't be surprised if his cousin marched over to add his opinion to whatever was wrong.

"We had an argument earlier," Payton explained. "Uncle Gregor thought the hand-fasting should come first. Monsignor Bourguignon insisted the Catholic rite should take precedence."

"Then we pointed out that not everyone in the wedding parties is Roman Catholic," Kenneth said testily when he joined the discussion. "Me in particular. What's more, my bride and I already had our marriage blessed by the Church of England weeks ago."

The cleric snorted derisively.

"So," Payton continued with a sigh. "We eventually reached an agreement that the Monsignor would bless the unions once the hand-fasting was done."

"I agreed because Cat would like the blessing of her grandfather's church," Kenneth said.

The priest adjusted his pince-nez. "However, I was unaware then that the rituals were to take place in a distillery. I must sanctify this sinful place."

Tavish bristled, but trying to win an argument about religion and whisky would simply make matters worse. "Go ahead then, Monsignor," he said. "Sprinkle yer holy water." He had a momentary urge to offer a bottle of *Uachdaran* for the task, but thought better of it.

～

ALBA BREATHED AGAIN once the priest had finished his blessing of the distillery. She'd been a Catholic since birth, but wanted to avoid any unpleasantness about religion. It was enough that Payton had readily agreed to raise their children in the true faith.

Her frantic heart calmed when her husband's uncle raised his arms. Everyone followed his lead when he turned to the east. "Blessed be this union with the gifts from the East—a new beginning, purity of the mind and body."

Payton had explained the ritual of hand-fasting to her, but the words still seemed very foreign.

Then, everyone turned with Gregor to face a different direction. "Blessed be this union with the gifts of the South, for passion and the warmth of a loving home. Share the fire within ye in even the darkest of times."

The fire within echoed in Alba's heart. She burned to lie abed naked exploring more of Payton's tempting body.

"Blessed be this union with the gifts of the West, for emotion. By hand-fasting, ye offer absolute trust to one another, and vow to keep yer hearts open in sorrow as well as joy."

The sentiment behind the words was beginning to make sense to Alba. She wasn't naive enough to believe she and Payton wouldn't experience dark times, but they'd have love to sustain them.

"Blessed be this union with the gifts of the North, sustenance, fertility and security. The earth will feed and enrich ye, and help ye to build a loving home."

Sí, her heart proclaimed. A loving home, filled with Payton's *niños*.

She marveled that the old Scot had uttered these sacred words from the heart, not from a book. "Perfect," she whispered.

"Aye," Payton replied hoarsely.

Gregor cleared his throat. "Payton King and Alba Castillero, I bid ye look into each other's eyes."

"I love ye," Payton mouthed as they obeyed, his green eyes full of the love he professed.

"Will ye honor and respect one another, and seek to never stain that honor?"

"We will."

Gregor draped his plaid over their joined hands.

"And so, the first binding is made," he declared. "Will ye share each other's pain and seek to ease it?"

"We will."

Payton removed the plaid draped over his shoulder and placed it alongside Gregor's.

"And so, the second binding is made. Will ye share the burdens so that yer spirits may grow in this union?"

"We will."

Tavish wound his plaid around their hands.

"And so, the third binding is made. Will ye share each other's laughter, and look for the brightness in life and the good in each other?"

"We will."

Lastly, Niven wound his plaid around their joined hands and knotted it loosely.

"And so, the fourth binding is made," Gregor declared. "Payton and Alba, as yer hands are bound together now, so yer lives and spirits are joined in a union of love and trust. Above ye are the stars and below ye is the earth. Like the stars, yer love should be a source of light and, like the earth, a firm foundation from which to grow."

Eyes sparkling, Payton pulled her to his body and they shared their first kiss as man and wife. There was nothing chaste about this kiss. Payton's tongue took possession of her mouth. She melted into his hard body and willingly let him breathe for her. Raucous cheers and applause echoed in her heart.

∽

ONCE GREGOR HAD COMPLETED the hand-fasting for Payton and Alba, he turned his attention to Cat and Kenneth. She filled her lungs, glad for the chance to fully appreciate the meaning of the ceremony while she listened and watched. She'd observed Gregor perform the rite for others in the past, but had never given much consideration to the words.

Her husband had fond memories of Tavish and Piper's hand-fasting in his London drawing room and had insisted on traveling to Scotland so his uncle could say the words over him and his bride. Now, she understood. She was especially grateful that her teary-eyed grandfather used his plaid for the final binding.

The notion of a Catholic blessing irked Kenneth, though he hadn't actually said as much. Alba's head was covered by her mother's beautiful lace mantilla, so Cat draped a plaid over her hair to appease the judgmental priest. Kenneth knelt beside her and she loved him all the more for it.

Both grooms became fidgety as the monsignor stretched out the rite. Kenneth even sighed irritably when a generous dousing of holy water was sprinkled over them. Cat feared Tavish might have a fit when the priest lit the censor and clouds of incense filled the air.

However, everyone present knew the Roman ritual meant a lot to Alba and to Cat's grandfather.

∼

PAYTON COULDN'T IMAGINE any place more suitable for his new life to begin. He might travel back and forth to London to conduct business for the family, but this was where he belonged. Another certainty filled his heart. Glengeárr was also where Alba belonged.

She was different. The black wedding dress that emphasized every lithe curve was just one example. She'd managed to explain the Andalusian style to Cat and Piper. However, Glengeárr could do with a touch of exotic spice. Perhaps that's what he loved about her. She inflamed him like no other woman ever had. But she also suited his temperament. She understood his humor, his moods. And there was that streak of Scottish stubbornness she'd inherited from her mother. In some ways, she was a puzzle. He intended to spend his life trying to figure her out, though the rational part of him acknowledged he never would. The joy would be in the effort.

CRIES OF JOY

Payton leaned close to Alba's ear. "I hope ye're nay disappointed," he whispered.

"Why would I be?" she replied, though she had an inkling of what her new husband meant.

"Piper's kitchen isna a very grand place for a wedding breakfast."

Alba considered her reply carefully. "If the French had not invaded my country and I had married in Spain, my parents would have thrown a lavish banquet in our *bodega*. Guests from all the neighboring *bodegas* in Jerez would have attended."

Regretting the frown that marred his handsome face, she hurried to explain. "However, I have married a man I love with all my heart. The guests at this kitchen table in a faraway corner of Scotland are all family. The only person missing is my father."

He took hold of her hand beneath the table. "But this is what he wanted. I think he kent before we did that we were meant to be together."

"No, *mi marido*, I knew as soon as I set eyes on you."

He trailed her hand up his kilt and placed it on his most intimate place. "Weel. I admit my brain thought ye were a lad, but my body told me ye were a lass. Still kens it, as ye can tell."

Tavish unexpectedly made a big show of clearing his throat. "I dinna intend to make a speech, except to say my brother clearly wishes to whisk his beautiful bride upstairs."

The heat rose in Alba's face, but Payton held her hand firmly in place on the warm flesh under his kilt.

Tavish grinned. "On second thought," he continued, raising his tumbler of *Uachdaran*. "Join me in toasting a courageous brother I'm proud of and his canny new wife. To Payton and Alba."

As the others echoed the toast, Alba was suddenly in Payton's arms.

"I thank ye, Tavish," he quipped. "For grantin' permission to begin my married life."

She anchored her arms around his neck as he carried her up the stairs accompanied by peals of laughter from below.

~

Payton lifted his bride over the threshold of the bedroom where he'd slept for years. When they were bairns, the three brothers shared the room. Tavish eventually got his own bedroom. After the deaths of their parents, each son got his privacy.

Payton had at one time thought he would be carrying

Catriona Neish into his lair. Funny how life could take unexpected twists and turns.

"A penny for your thoughts," Alba teased, jolting him back to the present.

He suddenly saw the cramped bedroom through his bride's eyes. "Ye ken this is only temporary."

"Temporary?" she replied.

Realizing he'd given the wrong impression, he strove to explain. "Livin' wi' Tavish and Piper. I'll build a cottage. Close by, but just for us, for ye."

She twirled a finger in his hair. "A place of our own will be good for our *niños*, but I'm content to live here in the meanwhile. Piper and I get along and I have already learned much about babies from helping her. You forget I've camped under the stars for years. You are part of this house and I've dreamt of lying with you in this bedroom."

He'd thirsted for hours to explore the tempting black gown and putting her down meant he'd wasted the opportunity. "Aye. 'Tisna very grand. We dinna have a gallery wi' portraits..."

She put a finger to his lips. "You've slept here since you were a boy."

"Aye."

"Then it's fitting this is where you'll make me your wife in every way."

His swollen cock saluted its approval of the prospect. "How do I get this lovely frock off ye?" he asked.

∽

"I have to admit," Alba whispered when the unfastened gown pooled at her feet. Gooseflesh marched over her naked skin. Her throat was too dry to tell Payton she was afraid, so she averted her gaze from the intense longing in his eyes. He'd already shucked his boots and removed most of his clothing. When the kilt went...

"Admit what?" he asked as the kilt fell to the floor.

She'd seen his prodigious lance before, even taken him into her mouth. But..."You're a big man," she murmured, her heart racing when he took himself in hand.

"I ken the good Lord was generous wi'..."

Frowning, he paused.

She'd disappointed him.

"I'm an insensitive fool," he said, gathering her close. "I ken ye're tiny, but I'll make ye ready. They say 'tis painful the first time, I canna deny it."

The reassuring warmth of his nakedness and the musky scent she loved eased her nervousness. They'd discussed intimate details of making love before when she'd craved his maleness inside her and he'd resisted her entreaties. "I'm already wet, down there," she confessed.

"Aye," he growled and I'll wager my little Spanish warrior will be even wetter soon."

She'd never really understood the reason for her mother's decision to wed Pedro Castillero and leave Scotland. When Payton carried her to the bed and began to suckle, she knew Olivia Castillero had been consumed with love for her handsome Spaniard.

PAYTON AND THE PASSIONATE PARTISAN

~

Payton kept telling himself to go slowly, but the intoxicating aroma of Alba's arousal had him in knots. His fingers itched to dip into the wetness she'd spoken of. He already anticipated the taste of her on his lips.

It might kill him, but he had to let her set the pace. In truth, suckling her tits was no hardship. He loved the way her nipples turned to hard little cobnuts neath his tongue.

A throaty groan and thrusting hips eventually let him know her woman's place wanted attention.

At last!

He parted her legs and knelt between them. This would be the last time he'd look at a virgin's opening. Dismissing that thought as likely to push him over the edge, he bent his head and suckled her juices, all the while squeezing her nipples.

It never took his passionate partisan long to spend and today was no exception. As she screamed her fulfillment, he lifted her hips, positioned himself and prayed he would do this right.

"Now, now, Payton," she gasped.

Needing no further encouragement, he thrust inside. She stopped breathing and cried out when he breached her maidenhead. He held still, desperately trying to ignore the protests from his greedy cock. As he'd expected, her sheath was mindbogglingly, wonderfully tight and hot. His hips wouldn't be still.

"*Te pertenezco ahora,*" she whispered. "I belong to you now."

"And I to you," he replied as his need took over and he thrust and withdrew, thrust and withdrew.

In the thrall of male urges beyond his control, he slowly recognized the signs of her arousal. She matched his rhythm stroke for stroke. His Alba had risen to the challenge and was taking the journey with him. When his seed erupted into her body, his wife's cries of joy echoed in his heart.

DIFFERENT PATHS

I n the days following Payton's wedding, Niven tried his best to enter into the joyous spirit of the celebrations. Kenneth hosted a gala dinner at Lockie House during which Piper and Tavish revealed they were expecting another bairn.

All in all, things in Glengeárr were looking up. Tavish now had Payton and Alba to assist with the expansion of the distillery. The folk of the tiny village were proud of the Regent's gold-edged shield and even prouder that they'd produced another duchess.

Yet, feelings of alienation plagued Niven. He itched to get back to London where he had a role to play. Withenshawe listened to his opinions. What he thought mattered. If he stayed in the Highlands, he'd end up married to a lass he didn't love. Or he'd become the aging bachelor uncle to his brothers' bairns—another Gregor. Much as he loved the old fart, the prospect filled him with dread.

When Kenneth and Cat took ship for London, he would sail with them and make his life there.

∽

IDLY WONDERING how long Justin was planning to leave her naked and tied to the enormous fourposter, Jasmine tamped down her growing arousal and let her gaze wander over the opulent bedroom.

Luxurious velvet drapery cloaked the massive windows. Priceless works of art adorned the walls. A hearty fire blazed in the hearth. She'd gradually come round to accepting his refusal to allow her scratched cedar chest to be brought from London. Indeed, she'd been forbidden to bring anything from her old life.

However, life in Berkshire was good. Justin was a generous husband. He'd arranged for her father to be barred from the London gaming houses and paid off her family's debts.

Her parents weren't allowed to visit the Berkshire estate, which was perhaps just as well. Her mother certainly wouldn't approve of the various pieces of apparatus she and Justin had in their bedroom.

She'd been shocked at first, but her husband had turned out to be just the sort of dominant man she needed.

Her body throbbed with anticipation when he finally appeared in the doorway, naked and with whip in hand.

∽

"Do you ever wonder about your former fiancée?" Alba asked, tracing her fingertips along her naked husband's thigh.

"'Tis a curious question to ask a *mon* who's just made love to ye," he replied sleepily.

She snuggled into his warmth, feeling the need to confess something ridiculous. "I worry about her."

He sat up and stared in disbelief. "To be honest, I ne'er give her a thought. She deserves whatever life has brought her."

"A rich husband, by all accounts, and a stately mansion."

"Waterdown canna be as rich as I am," he replied. "He doesna have ye."

"I hope she's happy," Alba whispered, coaxing him to lie down. "But I still think she was a fool to give you up."

"Weel, I already kent I didna love her, even before I met ye. Let's hope Carmichael cares for her. Now, enough talk o' Miss Foxworthy. On the morrow, we'll tour the fields hereabouts and choose a spot for our cottage."

"Too bad Niven and Kenneth are leaving. They could have helped you with construction."

"Aye," he replied wistfully. "However, Kenneth and Cat canna stay in Scotland. I dinna rightly ken what to say about Niven. I suppose he has to follow his own path."

Alba lay awake for a good while, contemplating the path her own life had taken. Leaving behind country and family had been a wrenching decision, but she wouldn't have wanted it any other way. Payton was her destiny. She belonged in his arms in this remote Scottish village.

DID YOU MISS TAVISH AND PIPER'S LOVE STORY?

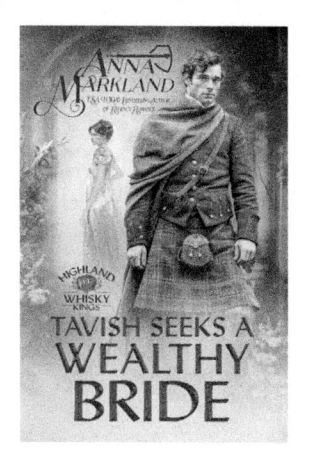

You can find *Tavish Seeks a Wealthy Bride* on Amazon.

Here's a wee excerpt:

"'Tis a sad truth that Glengeárr isna where ye'll find the wealth ye need. I'd venture to say ye willna find it in the whole o' Scotland."

"So, where is this wonderful Utopia full o' rich lasses?" Tavish asked his uncle.

"London," Gregor replied with a disturbing twinkle in his eyes.

"Surely, Uncle, ye dinna expect us to wed Sassenachs?" Tavish spluttered.

HISTORICAL FOOTNOTES

SPANISH SHERRY
https://www.sherrynotes.com/2013/background/sherry-production-process/

This website has an excellent diagram which explains the complicated process of making sherry.

https://www.sherrynotes.com/2013/background/sherry-solera-system/

An explanation of the solera system

https://www.sherrynotes.com/2013/background/flor-sherry-yeast/ For more on *flor*.

THE SPANISH ARMADA

https://www.britishbattles.com/the-spanish-war/the-spanish-armada/

Lengthy article with lots of detail.

http://www.thesonsofscotland.co.uk/thespanisharmadainscotland.htm

More about the Spanish ship wrecked near Tobermory on Mull.

GIBRALTAR

https://en.wikipedia.org/wiki/Strait_of_Gibraltar

https://en.wikipedia.org/wiki/Gibraltar

NAPOLEONIC INVASION OF SPAIN

https://en.wikipedia.org/wiki/Timeline_of_the_Peninsular_War#1812

A useful timeline. Check out Aug 25th 1812, the date French troops abandoned the siege of Cadiz. The last French garrison in Spain didn't surrender until June 4th 1814. Napoleon had abdicated the previous April.

GUERRILLA WARFARE IN SPAIN

I am indebted to Major Jose de la Pisa of the Spanish Marine Corps for his excellent dissertation on the Spanish resistance during the Peninsular War. https://apps.dtic.mil/sti/pdfs/ADA600639.pdf

FRENCH WEAPONRY

https://en.wikipedia.org/wiki/Gribeauval_system

GENERALISSIMO BALLESTEROS

I based this character on an actual historical figure, with a few adjustments!

http://www.historyofwar.org/articles/people_ballesteros_francisco.html

NOBLE EXPECTATIONS

If a commoner speaks to a duke or duchess, he is expected to address the noble as *Your Grace*. A fellow noble can use the other person's title. So, the enigmatic Earl of Waterdown feels entitled to address Maureen Hawkins as *Duchess*.

DOUSE MY TOPLIGHTS

Just one of Kenneth's curious outbursts. You may

recall *Dash my wig and trouser buttons* from Tavish Seeks a Wealthy Bride.

https://whynow.co.uk/read/susie-dents-top-tens-10-brilliant-swearwords

Printed in Great Britain
by Amazon